Lem glanced round again, closing the outer door before he dropped his voice to ask, 'Look, can you keep a secret?'

Belinda's fingers knotted in the Girl Guides' salute. 'Honour bright.'

'I am here,' announced [illegible] ntously, 'to book music lessons for Nigel C[illegible]

'Nigel who?' aske[illegible] atisfied smile from Lem's face [illegible]

'Nigel Coc[illegible] e're living up at the [illegible]

Beli[illegible] ics than the rock scene. S[illegible] had never heard Graf Spee, nor [illegible] rane until his purchase of the manor ho[illegible] household name in Churston Deckle. Or, in [illegible] of her father, a household curse. 'Oh, it's you,' sh[illegible] d.

'Right,' Lem nodded. 'So you see why our arrangements will have to be kept under wraps.'

'Not really.' Belinda shook her pretty head. Life in Churston Deckle had done little to familiarize her with the nuances of the music business . . .

ANGUS WELLS

Roll Over Beethoven

Based upon the Central Independent Television series by Laurence Marks and Maurice Gran

PANTHER
Granada Publishing

Panther Books
Granada Publishing Ltd
8 Grafton Street, London W1X 3LA

Published by Panther Books 1985

This publication is based on the television series *Roll Over Beethoven* produced by Central Independent Television plc.

ISBN 0-586-06600-4

Printed and bound in Great Britain by
Collins, Glasgow

Set in Times

1

Churston Deckle was one of those sleepy Surrey hamlets that seem to have hidden themselves away from the path of progress as seen by the civic planners. Far enough from major roads to deter the developers, from new towns to deter the factory owners, indeed, far enough from anywhere to deter almost everyone, Churston Deckle basked in tranquil self-satisfaction, the domain of maiden aunts and retired military gentlemen. Churston Deckle adhered with the tenacity of the symbolic bulldogs owned by several residents to the traditional virtues of the English Home Counties village. That is to say, the virtues as perceived and translated, if not dictated, by the same maiden aunts and retired military gentlemen who live in such places. For them, time stands still. In their atlases the larger part of the known world is coloured the glorious red of the long-dead British Empire. For them, there is honey still for tea and progress means the inclusion of 'colonial' players appearing in the visiting cricket elevens. Bees still buzz of a summer evening in the villages like Churston Deckle, and the gardens are immaculate as the cottages, neat, ivy-clad, rose-bedecked advertisement of their owners' standards: those of a quieter, more leisurely age, when people knew their places and were happy to be in them. Time's sole intrusions came in the form of the inevitably-bad news contained in the newspapers and the television aerials that semaphored from beside neat stone chimneys and thatched roofs. For most of Churston Deckle, the outside world existed only on television; and so far as most of the inhabitants were concerned, that was the best place for it.

Consequently, the purchase by Nigel Cochrane, rock star, of the Grange came – to put it in the genteel terms of Churston Deckle – as something of a surprise to those inhabitants most concerned with the maintenance of standards. To put it in Nigel's terms, the bleedin' busybodies were having a go at him because him being a millionaire rock star, he was the only one could afford the place. Unless some oil sheik had come along; which might well have caused even more consternation.

The Grange was a Georgian manor house in the Palladian style, an elegant creation commanding a view over the village from its vantage point atop a cunningly-wooded hillock. It was sufficiently distanced from its nearest neighbour, the cottage owned by Oliver Purcell, that the anticipated clamour of orgies, all-night parties, and deafening rock would have gone unnoticed had there been such clamour. That there was not was of little consequence to the protestors, chief amongst them, the tradition-conscious Mr Purcell. That Nigel occupied the Grange with only his faithful roadie, Lem, for company did nothing to dispel the rumours of debauchery concocted in the fertile imagination of the good citizen. Rock stars were rock stars, and we all know what rock stars get up to, don't we? Television and an occasional glance at the lower forms of newspaper whilst browsing in the village store had revealed all Oliver Purcell needed to know about Nigel Cochrane. That Nigel had bought the Grange to get away from all that was of no consequence to Mr Purcell, who, in any event, had not – nor ever would if he could help it – spoken to Nigel. In point of fact, Nigel had made his gold discs and his millions playing bass and singing lead with the heavy rock group, Graf Spee, and wanted to try making it on his own. To that end he had quit the group and bought the Grange with the idea of retiring there whilst recording a solo album on the equipment installed, at an expense that would have reduced his neighbour to apoplectic envy, prior to his arrival. As was not the case with most residents of Churston Deckle, Nigel could afford it. He could also afford a Jaguar, a Mercedes, a Porsche, and a Rolls Royce, all of which stood in the gravelled forecourt of the Grange awaiting his use, a fact noted and duly reported on by the postman, the milkman and any other casual visitor to the Grange, much to the outrage of Oliver Purcell.

Overlooking the cottage from his reclusive vantage point, Nigel was unaware of the furore his arrival caused. He had other things on his mind, his solo album amongst them. Indeed, chief amongst them: the reason he had had Lem find him this backwater mansion with its guaranteed seclusion. He had the place and he had the time; he had the equipment to record every sound he could synthesize from the array of keyboards lining the sound-proofed walls of his studio. He was all set up. Ready to go, save for one thing. Nigel Cochrane had only the skimpiest idea where to put his fingers on a keyboard: he needed piano lessons.

That this should be so was a source of embarrassment to Nigel great enough that it had much influenced his decision to retreat to Churston Deckle. There, protected by a gatekeeper and the natural reticence of the Home Counties, Nigel believed he could achieve his aim of establishing his solo magnificence once his problem was overcome. Which, in its turn, gave rise to another problem: how to achieve musical competence in secret. The idea of the music business discovering this unfortunate lack was a matter of some concern to the rock star, and so it fell, as usual, to the faithful Lem to provide an answer. Which he did with his customary ease and the help of the local Yellow Pages. There, ensconced between Mouldings (See also Architectural & General Joinery Mfrs: Plastics – Extrusion Mfrs: Plastics – Moulders) and Musical Instrument & Music Shops (See also Organ Dealers: Piano Mfrs & Dealers), he found a solitary music teacher in Churston Deckle itself. That the name of this music teacher was Belinda Purcell meant nothing to Lem. In those early days of rustic tranquility there was no reason why it should, so Lem simply ripped the relevant page from the directory and set out to make his master's arrangements with the prospective teacher.

As Lem descended from the Grange, Belinda was completing a lesson with a pre-pubescent pupil painted and plumed as a post-adolescent strumpet. And to Oliver's irritation the lesson had run over time, thus disrupting a routine he had carefully established over the years since the demise of his wife, a routine in which his daughter played a leading role as housekeeper, companion, and skivvy. It was an arrangement that suited Oliver admirably. Now, from the wheelchair to which he was wont, from time to time as the mood caught him, to retire, Oliver called complainingly.

'It's after eleven o'clock, Belinda. You cannot have failed to have heard the chimes if I, whose hearing was damaged by a German artillery barrage . . .'

'All right, Daddy.' Belinda looked up from the piano, smiling with fond resignation. 'Everyone knows you heeded your country's call in 1939.'

'Why?' Beside her, the teeny trollop peered curiously at the patrician old man in the wheelchair. 'What happened in 1939?'

'You'd better go now, Julie.' Belinda said it quickly,

ushering the girl out before Oliver had time to rise to the irresistible bait.

Oliver shook his head in disapproving disbelief as the child left.

'Did you see that? Lipstick! Dyed hair! High heels! And how old can she be? Twelve? Thirteen? I would never have let you dress like that when you were her age.'

'You still don't let me, Daddy.'

Belinda followed her father into the conservatory as he wheeled his way over to his plants.

'Someone has to maintain standards,' he informed her. Then, encouragingly, to a plant, 'Come on, Arnold,' and to Belinda again, 'I just thank the Lord that I retired from teaching when I did.'

'Oh, for heaven's sake, Daddy.' Belinda's soft reproval went unheard in the flow of rhetoric. 'Don't start that again.'

'I can pinpoint the exact moment the country began to go to the dogs.' Oliver busied himself with his plants as he spoke, not seeing his daughter parrot the words behind him. 'It was autumn term, 1963. I noticed it at the very first assembly. We were singing "All Things Bright and Beautiful" and half my boys were adding "yeah, yeah" at the end of every verse! Oh, Arnold, what have you been doing?' This to the plant. 'The entire sixth form were affecting Liverpool accents. Sprouting hair down to their shirt collars! And wearing Chelsea boots! All the fault of those damned Beatles! They set us on the slippery slope that led to Harold Wilson, the Common Market, decimalization.'

'I always thought the Beatles were rather sweet,' remarked Belinda, mildly.

'I wrote to *The Times*, you know,' grumped Oliver.

'You always do, Daddy.' Belinda had heard it all

before. Frequently. "Where is it all leading?" you demanded. They didn't print it. They never do.'

'I'll tell you where it's led,' announced Oliver, unperturbed and unstoppable once mounted astride a favourite hobbyhorse. 'To some damn' pop singer buying the Grange. One of the finest houses in the entire county! Why didn't the National Trust buy the place?'

'Probably because your damn' pop singer had more money than the National Trust,' Belinda suggested. 'Leave the poor chap alone.'

Which was not to be, for at that moment the representative of 'the poor chap' rang the doorbell.

What Belinda saw when she answered was a young man with a South London accent dressed pop group casual. She told him she didn't want any heather, then asked if he had come to fix the drains. What Lem saw was a young woman who was pretty without the aid of cosmetics, golden hair curling around an oval face dominated by clear blue eyes, dressed in soberly sensible wool and tweed. He established that she was, indeed, the music teacher described in the torn directory and that he wished to engage her services. More than a little bemused by his distinctly non-Churston Deckle approach, Belinda invited him into the drawing room where she gave her lessons.

'Oh, you got a Steinway.' Lem crossed to the piano and began to mimic playing.

'You're familiar with the piano?' Belinda stared at him with a mixture of curiosity and amazement.

'Familiar?' Lem's customarily cheerful face split in a broad grin. 'I was Barry Manilow's roadie for three years. Not that I want that mooted about! But I was strapped for child maintenance.'

Oliver's voice intruded querulously from the conservatory: 'Belinda! It's half-day closing and I'm down to my last Iron Jelloid.'

'My father,' Belinda explained.

'Oh, you don't live alone.' Lem sounded disappointed. Belinda wondered why. She asked, 'Tell me, Mister . . .?'

'Lem,' supplied Lem.

'For whom do you wish to book piano lessons?' she continued formally.

'It's my . . .' Lem glanced around as though afraid of being overheard. 'My boss. Do you do grown-ups?'

'Not usually.' Belinda went on staring at her extraordinary visitor, curiosity getting the upper hand now. 'But there's no rule against it.'

'So what's your rates?' asked Lem.

'Three hundred and fifty pounds a year,' said Oliver from the conservatory door. 'Which is outrageous when you consider they only empty the dustbins when the mood takes them. Has he come about the drains?'

'Daddy, I thought you were deaf today.' Belinda closed the door with her father on the far side.

'Where's my coffee?' came the plaintive reply.

'I'm sorry about that.' Belinda turned back to Lem. 'Actually, I charge £5 an hour, but if that's too much . . .'

'No sweat,' chuckled Lem. 'He's got more money than the Duke of Westminster.'

'Who has?' asked Belinda.

Lem glanced round again, closing the outer door before he dropped his voice to ask, 'Look, can you keep a secret?'

Belinda's fingers knotted in the Girl Guides' salute. 'Honour bright.'

'I am here,' announced Lem portentously, 'to book music lessons for Nigel Cochrane.'

'Nigel who?' asked Belinda, wiping the satisfied smile from Lem's face.

'Nigel Cochrane! Graf Spee! Rock 'n' roll! We're living up at the Grange.'

Belinda was more in tune with classics than the rock scene. So far as she was aware, she had never heard Graf Spee, nor of them or Nigel Cochrane until his purchase of the manor house made him a household name in Churston Deckle. Or, in the case of her father, a household curse. 'Oh, it's you,' she said.

'Right,' Lem nodded. 'So you see why our arrangements will have to be kept under wraps.'

'Not really.' Belinda shook her pretty head. Life in Churston Deckle had done little to familiarize her with the nuances of the music business.

'Look, doll.' Lem was taken aback by her ignorance of a fame he took for granted. 'Nigel splits the world's number one band to make a solo album. Big news in Rock City! So we would be extremely pissed off if the news leaks out that first he has to take piano lessons. That's why we selected an obscure little music teacher like your good self.'

Belinda might have been out of touch with what Lem regarded as the important things in life, but she had a sound sense, Home Counties bred, of the proprieties. Phrases such as 'pissed off' were not used in the Purcell drawing room; nor was she accustomed to hearing herself described in so truthfully disparaging a fashion. 'I'm thrilled to bits,' she said, sarcastically.

The sarcasm was lost on Lem, who grinned and said, 'So you should be. Right! The motor will be here for you at two, to fetch you up to the Grange.'

'Just a second, Mister . . .' Business was conducted in a more leisurely manner in Churston Deckle.

'Lem,' Lem supplied again. 'Two o'clock no good?'

'It's not that.' Belinda began to see signs of culture clash. My pupils visit me here.'

It was Lem's turn to be taken aback. This was not how rustic music teachers were supposed to react when graced with a summons from Nigel Cochrane. He stopped smiling to say, 'But Nige doesn't want no one seeing him.'

'I'm sorry.' Belinda smiled, shaking her head firmly. 'But my father's not as young as he used to be, and he was pretty old then. I can't possibly leave him alone.'

'Oh, strap me!' Lem recognized implacable obstinacy when it blocked his path to Nigel's desires. He could also compromise with an immovable object. In that respect, at least, he shared an Islamic practicality with Mohammed. 'All right. You solemnly swear you won't bunny to the press?'

'Sorry?' *Bunny* was not a term much used in Churston Deckle.

'Talk to the newspapers,' Lem elaborated.

'Under the circumstances,' promised Belinda solemnly, 'I won't even tell Daddy.'

'Honour bright?' grinned Lem.

'Honour bright,' agreed Belinda.

Unlike his prospective piano teacher, Nigel Cochrane had not enjoyed the benefits of a 'good' education. His accent belonged more to Streatham than to Surrey and his idea of relaxation was a pin-table rather than a piano. His millions were made from a musical talent that produced the kind of songs, delivered in the kind of voice, with the kind of backing that the pop purchasing public liked. He had no wish to disillusion his fans.

'You reckon we can trust her not to bunny to the

papers?' he asked Lem as his bass-player's fingers fluttered on the flippers of his pinball machine.

From across the opulent living room Lem nodded over the cork of a champagne bottle. 'Yeah. We're all right with her. After all, she hasn't heard of Graf Spee.'

'Leave off!' Shock lost Nigel a ball. 'She's winding you up.'

Lem shrugged, crossing the room as the cork popped to splash champagne into polystyrene cups and the pin-table.

'Lem!' Nigel yelped, jumping back. 'I've lost my free game now.'

The roadie ignored him, proudly producing two burgers from grease-stained paper bags.

'Dinner is served.'

Mollified, Nigel bit into a burger. And became instantly unmollified.

'Dinner is cold.'

It was too much for Lem: there were limits to which even the most superlative superstar could push the most faithful of followers. 'It's not my fault, man,' he complained. 'Pop down to the nearest MacDonalds, you said. Do you know where that is? Dorking! Bloody miles!'

Nigel sighed, knowing that rural retreat was not his friend's idea of fun. 'Just stick it all in the microwave, okay?' he suggested, watching Lem open the front of a converted Louis XVI escritoire to produce the warning, 'Not the champagne, Lem. That's warm enough already.'

'Hold tight, Nige. I'm used to room service.' Lem closed the microwave-cum-escritoire. 'I mean, on the road we had everything on tap. Booze. Food. Depraved adolescent girls.'

'Those days of wanton, mindless excess are over, Lem.' Nigel assumed an expression of ascetic severity that faded as he sipped the champagne. 'Couldn't you get vintage?'

'Yeah, but I thought that was a bit wanton.' Lem regained his good humour. He needed it to handle his employer's moods.

'So what time are you collecting this piano teacher?' Nigel asked.

'I forgot to tell you.' Lem obeyed the warning buzz of the microwave to extract the burgers. 'She's not coming up here, Nige. You've got to go down to her pad.'

It had the effect he was expecting. A look of panic overpowered Nigel's face and he sank into a padded armchair with creaking leather pants.

'Lem!' It was a wail of protest. 'I'm trying to keep a low profile.'

'It's all right, Nige,' Lem soothed. 'She's cool.'

But Nigel was not to be so easily placated. He began to chew his fingernails, managing to sound muffled and petulant at the same time. 'I just need the rest of the band hearing I'm taking music lessons. They got it in for me as it is. They'll crucify me! Why can't she come up here?'

''Cos she's got this daft old dad to look after,' Lem explained. 'Don't worry, Nige. She don't know you from Adam Ant.'

'All I can say is,' said Nigel, 'she must be quite old.'

'She is,' Lem agreed solemnly. 'She must be nearly as old as us.'

As apprehension mounted in the Grange, so did discord in the Purcell cottage. Oliver was in the conservatory, awaiting the arrival of his afternoon tea, which, as was the case with all those things in his life over which he exerted control, was a regular procedure scheduled according to a strict timetable. But today that ordered regularity was disrupted. Oliver could sense it as Belinda set down the tray. He sniffed, then sniffed again as he lifted the lid of the teapot.

'This is common or garden Indian tea,' he bristled. 'Where's my Earl Grey?'

'Mr Daventree no longer stocks it, Daddy.' Belinda's voice was patient, accustomed to such petulance in much the same way as Lem. 'He says it's not worth it for just one customer.'

'Not worth it?' Oliver's brisk moustache bristled along with his annoyance. 'Change and decay in all around I see.' He turned to study his daughter for dramatic effect and abruptly changed tack. 'Belinda, are you wearing rouge and pancake?'

Any hint of cosmetics was rouge and pancake to Oliver Purcell: the mark of a scarlet woman.

'I have applied the merest touch of make-up, yes,' said Belinda with mild defiance.

'Touch?' barked Oliver with exaggeration. 'You have that muck half an inch thick all over your face.'

'I just want to make a reasonable impression,' Belinda countered nervously. 'My new pupil happens to be an adult.'

'You mean a man!' Oliver pounced dog-like on the threatening bone of liberation.

'A male adult, yes,' conceded Belinda.

'I forbid you to teach him.' Imperiously.

'Don't be silly. He's paid for twenty lessons in advance. A hundred pounds.'

'A hundred pounds?' In Oliver's outdated world this was massive extravagance. 'In my day only one sort of man gave a woman that sort of money. And only one sort of woman accepted it. The sort of woman who wore make-up! Your mother never wore make-up.'

'You never let her, Daddy.' Said with fond exasperation.

Oliver was about to add more, disturbed by these unsuspected tones of defiance, but the doorbell cut him short. Belinda left him fuming to open the door on Lem and a strange, hunched figure clad in leather jeans and a flying jacket worn over the head. She leapt back as the figure rushed inside and Lem cast a nervous glance back at the deserted street and the Rolls Royce parked ostentatiously outside the cottage before slamming the door as though afraid a baying pack of rabid reporters might follow him in. The figure halted just short of a collision with the far wall and dropped the flying jacket to reveal a mop of long, curly hair and a winning smile beneath dark glasses.

'Now do you recognize him?' asked Lem as the figure posed self-consciously.

'No,' said Belinda.

'Do you reckon he's Ronnie Biggs with a hair transplant?' Such ignorance was exasperating.

'Lem, it's cool,' Nigel intervened, turning the smile that had captivated millions on Belinda. 'You really don't know who I am?'

'Perhaps if I could see your eyes?'

'Glasses!' chortled Lem, seeing the solution and removing the offending objects.

'Perhaps not,' said Belinda.

'He wears them when he wants to be inconspicuous,' explained Lem.

'Inconspicuous?' Belinda studied the unfamiliar features; they were pleasant in a lumpy kind of way. 'In leather trousers and cowboy boots in Churston Deckle?'

'You got a point there.' Nigel frowned, considering it for the first time. 'Why didn't you think of that, Lem?'

The roadie gasped. 'I was the one who talked him out of the lurex jacket.'

'Shall we get on with the first lesson?'

Belinda took refuge in the familiarity of polite brusqueness, prompting an admiring, 'Cool,' from her new pupil.

'Well, since you won't be needing me for a few minutes, I think I'll walk down to the village,' Lem said. 'The girls' school's having netball practice. See you later.'

He took his jacket, leaving the lanky Nigel standing vaguely embarrassed beside the equally awkward Belinda.

'So where's the joanna?' Nigel asked.

'Through there.' Belinda pointed the way to the drawing room. 'But before we go through, I ought to warn you it's best my father doesn't find out who you are. He doesn't really approve.'

'They never do,' murmured Lem from the doorway.

Oliver chose that moment to emerge from the conservatory, braking his wheelchair violently as he caught sight of Nigel's long hair and leather pants.

'Good God, a socialist!'

'Blimey,' gasped Nigel, taken equally aback, 'a Dalek!'

Recognition dawned on Oliver's face, transforming it to a mild puce that grew deeper as he bellowed, 'It's that damn' caterwauling pop singer I signed a petition against!'

'He's only come for a piano lesson, Daddy.' Belinda was embarrassed.

'Get out of my house!' ordered Oliver.

'Right, that's it.' Nigel twitched, his expression pained. 'Bad vibes. Lem, let's go.'

Lem moved protectively past his boss to confront the irate Oliver.

'We don't want that sort of aggro. We've got enough trouble with the Inland Revenue.' He dropped the flying jacket back over Nigel's head and turned to Belinda.

'Now be a good girl – next time you come to our place, eh?'

Bemused, Belinda nodded as the roadie guided the shuffling pop star out of the cottage and into the Rolls. The puce fading gradually to a mere flush, Oliver propelled himself to his writing desk, where he commenced the composition of a letter that had come suddenly to his devious and outraged mind.

'Sir,' he told himself, 'It is lamentable enough when one of the finest country houses in England falls into the grasp of a pop singer. How much more offensive it is to discover that Nigel Cochrane, the leather-clad crooner in question, is so incompetent a musician that he has to seek music tuition before he can embark on his next magnum opus. And to think the man is a millionaire! I am, sir, your obedient servant.'

He sat back, satisfied with his effort. 'I'll send that to *The Times*. Better still, I'll send it to the local paper and get it published.'

His flush faded to a more usual ruddiness, he proceeded to transcribe his composition to paper. And so began the tribulations of Nigel Cochrane, tribulations that would, in the end, have the opposite effect to that planned by Oliver.

If, in the eyes of Oliver Purcell, the intrusion of two denizens of the pop world into the placid routines of the village signified impending chaos, a disruption of standards and a general outrage, their presence also indicated change to his daughter. But where Oliver had no wish for change, being quite content with his life as he had organized it, Belinda saw in the advent of the larger world a chance to break free of a routine that, whilst accepted as inevitable, was neither her choice nor at all exciting. Her two brief meetings had suggested that Nigel and Lem lived a life quite incredibly different to the humdrum to which she had, over the years of looking after her father, become resigned, and so, with a fine if somewhat nervous determination, she ignored Oliver's dictates and duly presented herself at the Grange for the first lesson.

She was impressed by the uniformed gatekeeper who ushered her and her bicycle through the ornate gates and surprised to discover that Nigel and Lem occupied the vast house on their own. Lem opened the doors to her knock and led her into the manor, its Georgian elegance newly decorated, the furnishings modern and vastly expensive, such practical items as chairs and tables interspersed with electronic toys and machinery with which she was quite unfamiliar.

'How the other half lives,' she remarked, studying the paintings, one in particular catching her eye. A Van Gogh. 'Is that an original?'

'Course.' Lem hung her coat on a Brancusi sculpture. 'No investment potential in reproductions, Nige always says.'

'It's beautiful,' she remarked, impressed.

'Yeah, nice innit?' Lem agreed cheerfully. 'We won it playing darts with Stevie Wonder.'

'But isn't he . . .?' Belinda was sufficiently in touch with popular music to remember that Stevie Wonder wore dark glasses and was, so far as she recalled, blind. 'I hope you gave him a start.'

'We told him we had,' grinned Lem, leading her on to stand before a wall decorated with gold and silver discs. 'And these are the fruits of victory.'

'Nigel's pop group must have sold a lot of long players.'

There was less awe in the reaction than Lem had anticipated: he had yet to grow accustomed to Home Counties reserve. 'We done all right,' he nodded.

Belinda smiled politely and asked, 'Lem, were you actually *in* the group? You always say "we" . . . I mean, do you play an instrument?'

'Not as such, no.' Lem remained as serious as he was able. 'I was Nige's equipment manager and joint-roller. Mind you, I was featured heavily on one album track.'

'Doing what?' Belinda asked.

'Handclapping,' Lem informed her.

He appeared rather proud of that contribution, which rather confused Belinda so that she changed the subject, indicating a photograph of a darkly beautiful woman with jaw-to-jaw teeth pinned to a dart board, where it had obviously been used as a target.

'She's very pretty. Who is she?'

'Yeah.' Lem's mouth turned down as he followed Belinda's gaze. 'That's Crazy Laura.'

'A friend of Nigel's? Is she a musician?'

'No way.' Lem shook his head emphatically. 'She was a model on an album cover. She started on the sleeve and ended up in his trousers.'

Belinda blushed with embarrassment, grateful that Nigel chose that moment to saunter into the room. He had toned down his appearance, the leather pants replaced by equally tight, but at least not leather, jeans, offset by a black tee shirt adorned with a heavy silver skull and a pale blue overshirt.

'Hi,' he greeted her, smiling. 'Sorry I've kept you hanging on, only I've been talking to California.'

In Belinda's world a call to Dorking was something of an event. All she could think of to say was, 'All of it?'

'What a card!' chortled Lem.

'I've got a very wide circle of friends.' Nigel glared frostily at the chuckling Lem. 'See you later, Lem.'

'Yeah, all right.' Lem knew how to take a hint. 'I'll go for a spin in the jacuzzi.'

'Well, don't eat crisps in it this time,' warned Nigel. 'It blocks the filter.'

'Is the jacuzzi another one of your cars?' Belinda enquired.

'Nice one!' chuckled Lem.

'Not exactly. It's more sort of . . .' He seemed as awkward as Belinda felt, not confident of his ground in the face of her neat suit and demure imitation pearls. 'Shall we get down and do that funky thing?'

Following Lem's comments on Laura and her vague general idea of the depraved nature of a pop star's life, Belinda felt momentarily panicked by what she assumed was some super-casual invitation. Nervously, she said, 'Don't you think we should stick to music?'

'Yeah, that's what I meant.' Nigel was confused now. 'What did you think I meant?'

'After some of the things I've read in the papers,' she began.

But Nigel cut her short with a weary sigh: 'Look, that's all ancient history. I'm a grown-up; I'm a rate payer. What I want to do now is become accepted as a serious musician and creator of concept albums.' There was no irony in his tone as he led her over to a Fairlite synthesizer explaining, 'I have ordered a piano, but they're taking ages spraying it to match the carpet. So we'll have to make do with this.'

Belinda sat where indicated, studying what she assumed to be some variety of modern upright piano. 'That's all right.' Then she fingered a scale on the keyboard and jumped in fright as the blare of a brass band erupted from the speakers. 'Crumbs! What is it?'

'It's a synthesizer.' Nigel took it for granted, adjusting the sound selector keys to produce a wailing akin to bagpipes. 'Sorry, wrong setting.' He altered the controls again, this time producing a sound similar to a piano-harpsichord. 'Funny, ain't it?'

'I thought you said you couldn't play.' Belinda heard arpeggios emerge under his fingering.

'I can't,' he agreed dolefully. 'I was a red hot bassist, mind you. I invented the two best riffs of the decade. Otherwise, I just know enough chords to work out my songs.'

Whereupon he launched into the opening bars of 'What Did I See In You?', prompting Belinda to ask, 'Is that one of yours?'

'Yeah.' He stopped playing as though ashamed of the tune.

'Why have you stopped playing?'

'Well, it's crap,' he muttered. 'Ain't it?'

'How can I tell?' she asked reasonably. 'I haven't heard it yet. Why don't you play it for me?'

'I thought you'd never ask.'

He said it jokingly, but Belinda sensed that there was an underlying seriousness because he promptly went into the song:

'What did I see in you
That brought me through from spring to summer?
And as our time unfolds
Our simple songs have grown together.
Magic in the air,
Why should I dream?

What did I see in you?
What did I feel in you?
What did I find that brought me

To my childhood's end?
To start my life again.
To start my life again.'

The final notes died away and he turned to face her.

'What do you reckon?'

'It's lovely.' Belinda was impressed. There was real talent behind the self-doubt and the rock star petulance. 'Though I'd change that natural to a diminished.'

Nigel stared at her, incomprehension writ large on his knobby features, so she demonstrated.

'Yeah, that's nice,' he said admiringly. 'It's a really up-market chord, that one. The rest of the band will freak out when they hear that.'

'You seem terribly worried about what the rest of your group think of you,' she remarked. 'I thought you'd left them.'

'I have,' said Nigel, 'but I still want to impress them. I want my first solo album to come as a huge surprise. They think I'm a total wally. They don't think I can do it.'

'Of course you can do it, Nigel.' Belinda's tone was that of a piano teacher encouraging a doubtful pupil. 'Now shall we start with the scale of C major?'

'Is that the one without the black notes?' asked Nigel innocently.

He never got started because Lem burst into the room, a towel knotted about his waist and a ghetto blaster pressed to his ear. 'Cop an earful of this,' he suggested, setting the radio down so they could hear the DJ.

'. . . since Graf Spee split and Nigel Cochrane came back to England. So what has this reclusive superstar been up to?'

'I'm not reclusive,' Nigel complained. 'I just don't go out much.'

'Of course, he's working on his solo album,' said the

DJ. 'But first, we hear, Nigel is having to take – wait for it – music lessons! Talk about "Roll Over Beethoven"! But let's remember Nigel with Graf Spee, doing what he does best – playing bass.'

Heavy rock exploded from the ghetto blaster, introduced by a thunderous bass riff. Belinda rose from the bench she was sharing with Nigel as he exchanged a look with Lem and both men turned faces as explosive as the riff in her direction. The secret was a secret no longer. And, so far as the inhabitants of the Grange were concerned, Belinda was the betrayer. She began to back away as they moved menacingly towards her.

Basking in the warm glow of self-satisfaction, Oliver sat before his fireplace with the local paper and a pair of scissors. Neatly, he cut out his letter, reading it with visible pride until the slamming of the front door startled him and he slipped the cutting guiltily into his breast pocket.

'And to think the man is a millionaire,' he murmured as a furious Belinda stormed into the drawing room.

'I have never in my life been spoken to in such a way,' she announced furiously.

'Something the matter, dear?' he asked innocently.

'That dreadful pop singer accused me of telling some commercial radio station . . .'

'What on earth is a commercial radio station?' So far as Oliver was concerned, the BBC held a global monopoly on airwaves.

Belinda ignored the query, carried along by her anger. 'He said I did it for the publicity! That I wanted people to know I was teaching *him*!'

'I always said he'd turn out to be a thoroughly bad egg, my dear,' Oliver murmured complacently, hiding his delight.

'Don't you find it wearying, always being right?' Belinda snapped.

'Did once,' her father allowed, 'but now I'm used to it.'

'It was probably someone in the village.' Belinda slumped into an armchair. 'It was a rotten thing to do.'

'Rotten?' Oliver was surprised. 'I thought it was a public spirited act.'

Realization dawned as Belinda recognized the smug expression on her father's face.

'*You* telephoned that radio station, didn't you?'

'Certainly not.' Oliver was emphatic. 'As if I'd deal with one of the institutions responsible for the decline of this great country.'

His protest was belied by his next action: he tugged a handkerchief from his breast pocket, sending the cutting fluttering to the carpet, from whence Belinda seized it, her suspicions confirmed.

'Then what should I make of this?' she demanded.

'Mice?' suggested Oliver.

'With scissors?'

'Oh, very well.' Crossly. 'I've nothing to be ashamed of. I wrote to the local newspaper. I did it for the good of the whole community.'

'I hope you realize you may have blighted Nigel's entire career.' There were times Belinda wondered where the limits of her patience were set.

'Do you really think so?' asked Oliver hopefully. 'Where's my coffee?'

There was no reply: Belinda was already phoning the Grange.

'I'll be making a statement through my record company,' said Nigel.

'Please don't hang up,' asked Belinda, 'this is Belinda.'

'Goodbye.'

'Daddy thought he was acting for the best.'

'What's Daddy got to do with it?'

'He wrote to the local paper about you.'

'Oh. Well, tell him he's a devious old bastard.'

'There's no need to adopt that tone of voice.' Belinda's loyalties were divided. It was a feeling to which she would grow accustomed. 'I'm sorry you've been inconvenienced.'

'Inconvenienced?'

'Well, I just thought apologies were in order.' Primly. 'Good evening.'

'Yeah, all right. Sorry I lost my rag,' Nigel said into the dead telephone. 'Hello?'

He realized he was holding a disconnected phone and set it down. 'That was thingy. Belinda.'

'Thingy Belinda,' said Lem. 'Supergrass.'

'It's a shame about her,' remarked Nigel forlornly. 'I was really beginning to fancy her an' all.'

'Oh,' grinned Lem, 'so the stuff Crazy Laura put in your tea's starting to wear off, is it?'

'Don't you think she can look quite tasty?' Nigel wondered.

'Tasty?' Lem was confused.

'And sort of real,' said Nigel, wistfully.

Lem stared at his boss in wonderment. 'Look, you honestly reckon you can pull a bird like that after the way you slagged her off this afternoon? No chance, mate!'

'All right, all right,' grumbled Nigel. Then, brighter: 'Bet I can.'

'You're on,' said Lem.

'Cos I've still got that certain charisma,' continued Nigel. 'Haven't I? What was it that *Melody Maker* interview said? "The smouldering sexiness of a bruised cherub."'

‘All right.’ Lem sensed the chance of excitement. In Churston Deckle almost anything would rate as excitement. ‘And if the smouldering etcetera cherub cops out and I win?’

‘If I blow it, I’ll let you sing on the next album,’ promised Nigel.

‘Done,’ said Lem.

For a geranium, Arnold was looking a little below par as Oliver checked the plant’s foliage, following the advice given by so many tenders of growing things, if in his own somewhat eccentric way. He talked to his plants. As an Army officer might talk to a mob of untrained recruits.

‘Now pull yourself together, Arnold, and let’s have no more of this mildew nonsense. What’s that? Too much water? I’ll be the judge of that, sir, if you don’t mind.’ He glanced up as Belinda entered the conservatory bearing his morning coffee. ‘Hello, Belle. Just giving Arnold a good old talking to.’

‘Your morning coffee,’ Belinda announced.

‘I hope it’s . . .’

His daughter finished the sentence for him: ‘Dark roast Costa Rican, medium ground, with one spoonful of Demerara sugar and a dash of cream.’

‘Spot on,’ Oliver approved enthusiastically.

‘No,’ said Belinda. ‘It’s instant.’

‘But, Belle.’ Oliver sounded hurt. ‘You know I can’t abide instant coffee.’

‘Of course I know, Daddy,’ said Belinda with ominous calm.

‘She’s still cross with me, isn’t she, Arnold?’ Oliver asked the geranium.

‘Seething, Daddy,’ Belinda agreed.

Oliver decided that attack was the most profitable form

of defence: 'Now look here, my girl. I brought you up to be a good loser, so you just snap out of it. Why don't you play for me like you used to when you were a little girl?'

'That's how you'd like to keep me, isn't it?' Belinda demanded, unable to contain her bitterness any longer. 'A little girl. Every time a man enters my life in any way, you have to carry out your acts of petty sabotage. That's why you were so horrible to Nigel. Because you were frightened I found him . . . I might find him . . . attractive.'

'Attractive?' Oliver could scarcely believe these words came from his beloved Belinda. 'That yobbo? He could never be good enough for you!'

'Prince Andrew wouldn't be good enough for me,' retorted the object of his concern.

'Certainly not,' agreed her father. 'The company he keeps!'

'God, Daddy!' Belinda shook her head in hopeless exasperation. 'You're beyond belief.'

She went into the drawing room, where she sat down at the Steinway and began to finger the chords of 'What Did I See In You?', elaborating the simple melody to a pseudo-classicism.

'That's better, Belle,' encouraged Oliver, seeking to re-establish his comfortable status quo. 'You know, we're very contented together, you and I. What is that? Brahms? Debussy?'

'Neither.' Belinda decided to enjoy herself a little. 'It's Nigel Cochrane. You know – that damn yobbo.'

Oliver hid his confusion behind his cup. Then grimaced as he tasted the instant coffee.

'I'll make my own blasted coffee!' He stood up, wincing exaggeratedly. 'I didn't want to say anything, but I've been in dreadful pain all day. Shrapnel must be on the move. Wouldn't be surprised if it rained tomorrow.'

Belinda ignored the pathos, smiling in triumph as her father stumped out to the kitchen, his exit accompanied by further variations on the theme of Nigel's song.

She started as the composer came in through the conservatory door and said, 'Hello. You're playing my song.'

He looked apologetic, but Belinda was not yet ready to concede any victories, so she said, 'No I'm not.'

'Well, it sounded like it,' said Nigel, hurt.

'It sounds like a lot of songs.' Belinda remained cool. 'It's very derivative.'

'Well,' said Nigel, 'it's the life I've led.'

'What are you doing here?' she asked.

'I've come to apologize.' Nigel produced a massive cluster of red roses from behind his back. 'So I brought you some flowers.'

'With your money, that's an easy way of saying sorry.' But the size of the bunch still impressed her.

'Well, I brought them myself, I didn't ring Interflora,' Nigel told her defensively. 'I walked here.'

'What? All the way from the Grange?' Now she began to feel genuinely impressed.

'No.' Nigel looked surprised at the suggestion. 'From the limo.'

Belinda decided to be appeased. 'How many are there?' she asked.

'Ninety-nine,' smiled Nigel.

'Why not a hundred?'

'Well,' he shrugged, 'I don't want to be that flash.'

'And I don't want to be that easy.' Belinda smiled at him. 'I'll take two dozen.'

2

Belinda smiled as an uncomfortable-looking schoolboy asked to be excused at the end of his lesson.

'Of course. Run along home, then.'

'No, Miss.' The child fidgeted with embarrassment. 'I want to do a pee.'

'Oh, I see.' She turned to call up the stairs, 'Daddy, have you nearly finished?'

Muffled and irritable, Oliver's voice answered from on high. 'No, I have not.'

'I'm sorry, Miles.' Belinda laughed fondly as the discomfited youngster rushed helplessly away, then called again, 'Are you sure you're all right?'

'Of course I'm all right,' grumped Oliver. 'Can't a chap have a little privacy?'

'It's just that you've been up there for half an hour,' she replied.

'It gets harder as you get older, Belle,' her father retorted. 'Now I wish you'd let me alone to concentrate.'

Belinda shrugged and went back into the drawing room, preparing to light the fire as she heard a door close above her and the sound of footsteps on the stairs. A moment later Oliver came into the room with a cry of 'Eureka! Nearly stumped me with fourteen down, but I'm a wily old fox.' Triumphantly, he brandished *The Times* he was holding, displaying the completed crossword.

'Perhaps,' remarked Belinda, 'but poor little Miles had a more urgent need to visit your lair.'

'Beg pardon?' Oliver frowned incomprehendingly.

'I expect he'll be impersonating the fifth little piggy by now.'

Oliver's face assumed an expression of concentration as he began to recite the nursery rhyme. 'This little piggy went to market. This little piggy . . .'

'I fear for his flannels,' Belinda told him.

'Oh.' Oliver settled unconcerned in a chair. 'Wee wee.'

'Why,' Belinda enquired, 'do you insist on doing the crossword in the loo?'

'Furthest place from your tone deaf pupils,' grunted Oliver, the thought prompting him to check the date on his newspaper, the checking prompting in turn a look of horror. 'Good God! It's Friday again.'

'No one's denying it,' agreed Belinda.

'It's today that Visigoth comes to pound your keyboard and contaminate my home.'

'If you mean Nigel,' said Belinda mildly, 'Yes, he is due this afternoon.'

'Nigel, indeed!' Oliver's tone was disapproving. 'In my day we didn't presume to use first name terms after a mere fortnight. Your mother was still addressing me in public as Mr Purcell, three years after you were born. I prefer not to breathe in what he breathes out. I shall struggle down to the village and collect my pension.'

'He's coming for a piano lesson,' rebuked Belinda, 'Not to vandalize the telephone.'

'Lesson?' barked her father. 'Take the advice of one who was a professional teacher all his life. That yobbo is ineducable.'

'He's very diligent,' Belinda argued.

'Diligent he may be,' snorted Oliver, 'but his intentions are dishonourable.'

'Oh.' Belinda sounded pleased. 'Do you really think so?'

'I insist you wipe that smirk off your face immediately,' commanded Oliver.

Up at the Grange Nigel was struggling with a synthesized Mendelssohn Nocturne as he heard his Porsche growl to a halt and a cheerfully dishevelled Lem ambled into the room, looking the better for a night's debauchery.

'Do you know what time it is?' demanded the rock star. 'Why didn't you come home last night? What have you been doing?'

'That's funny.' Lem peered at Nigel, wondering if the solitude was getting to him. 'I better check me birth certificate.'

'You what?' Nigel frowned.

'I'm sure it didn't have your name in the space for Father,' grinned Lem.

'Your bloody birth certificate don't have no one's name in the space for Father,' snapped Nigel.

'You should have been there.' Lem flopped on to a sofa and proceeded to remove his shoes prior to collapsing full-length.

'I know!' Nigel was irritable. 'It was my invite.'

'Elton asked after you,' Lem told him, 'and Rod flew in especially. And there was some absolutely incredible chicks there.'

Nigel ignored embellishments: 'And who said you could take the Porsche? I fancied a quiet pint down the local last night and I had to take the Roller. It was very embarrassing.'

'My heart bleeds, Nige.' Somehow Lem didn't sound serious. 'You remember that tart you had in New York?'

'What?' Nigel was thrown by the sudden change of tack.

'You know,' elaborated Lem. 'The one who worked as a layout artist. Very apt job, I always thought. Zoe.'

'Oh, Zoe.' Nigel dredged a dim memory from the recesses of his mind. 'Yeah.'

'You had a very deep and meaningful relationship one weekend.'

'What about her?' Nigel was impatient.

'She was there.' Lem winked lasciviously. 'Very friendly.'

'You're an animal, Lem.' Nigel's face screwed itself into an expression of prim disapproval. 'I just thank heaven that I no longer share your essentially hedonistic sexual philosophy.'

'Been watching Channel Four again?' Lem relaxed against the cushions, basking in the warm glow of memory.

'Bugger all else to do on my own all last night,' grumbled Nigel.

'Why didn't you stay down the pub?' Lem asked.

'Because of the autograph hunters,' Nigel explained.

'What about them?' asked Lem.

'There weren't any.'

The roadie chuckled unsympathetically. 'You could have watched one of my tapes.'

'Your tapes!' Nigel was scornful in his new-found asceticism. 'That's filth, that is, Lem. We aren't all obsessed with strange sexual practices.'

'Makes the world go round,' leered Lem.

'There's more to life than sweaty bodies writhing in an orgy of lust,' Nigel pronounced.

'You don't say!'

'Anyway, the machine was on the blink.'

'You know your trouble?' Lem stared at his boss. 'That Miss Goody Two Shoes who teaches you piano.'

Nigel drew himself up to his full lanky height, his expression of disapproval oddly akin to Oliver's. 'I'd rather Belinda's name was not mentioned in the same breath as "Snow White And The Seven Perverts" if you don't mind, Lem.'

'You know you're never gonna pull that, don't you?' Lem warned.

The casual comment got to Nigel and he moved menacingly towards his friend. 'I'll have you!'

'You'd have more chance.' Lem leapt from the chair as Nigel approached. 'Frustration does strange things to a man.'

Nigel glared at him, genuine anger showing now. 'Just 'cos we've been together for ten years, it don't mean there are not boundaries beyond which you should not push your luck, my son.'

'You just don't like my singing voice,' Lem retorted. 'Do you?'

'Eh?'

Nigel halted his advance, confused. Lem said, 'Don't flannel. You know very well you bet me either you'd crack this Belinda or you'd let me sing on your new album.'

'That was then!' Nigel sounded aggrieved. 'She happens to be a bit special. All right?'

'Cool it, Nige.' Lem recognized the boundaries and drew back before he crossed them. 'I'm only winding you up. I know she's a lady. I know she's a bit church choir and home-made jam, and that's why I know I'll win the bet. 'Cos she's not gonna come across for a toerag like you. Breakfast?'

That the situation had changed in some subtle and, to Nigel, indefinable way was clear. What had begun as a potentially amusing pursuit of a challenging woman had now become something else. He was not certain what it had become, but he knew that he looked forward to his music lessons for other than professional artistic reasons, and his annoyance with Lem's casual lewdness had been genuine. It would have been easy for him to fill the manor house with willing groupies, but – apart from his paranoid desire to keep his musical inadequacies out of the limelight – he didn't want to. He wanted to concentrate on Belinda Purcell. Nigel had always been rather obsessional.

'That's much better,' said Belinda as he executed the Nocturne he had practised. Then: 'Oh dear. Famous last words.'

Nigel heard the muffed notes fade and held up his hands with a look of disgust.

'Look at them! Bunches of anarchic bananas.'

'No, Nigel. It's just a question of fingering. Look.'

She demonstrated, her left hand brushing his right as she played. She snatched it away as though burned and Nigel attempted the exercise again, this time succeeding. Belinda said, 'Much better,' approvingly.

'Actually,' Nigel remarked, 'that's quite a nice little riff.'

'Riff?' It was an unfamiliar term.

'Yeah.' Nigel picked the notes again.

'Oh,' Belinda smiled her understanding. 'You mean the motif.'

'Riff, motif,' Nigel shrugged, 'Same difference. Could build that up into a nice little number. Who's it by? Mendelssohn? I've heard of him. Hang about! He's dead isn't he?'

'Felix Bartholdy Mendelssohn,' Belinda supplied. '1809 to 1847.'

'Thought so.' Nigel grinned, pleased with himself. 'Great! He won't want a cut of the publishing then. Funny name, innit? Bartholdy.'

Belinda laughed. Nigel liked the sound. He also liked sitting close to her on the practice bench.

'So, er, do you reckon I'm making some progress?'

'Yes, you're doing very well,' Belinda nodded. 'You're nearly as good as some of my nine-year-olds.'

'Oh, great.' Nigel looked downcast. 'That really sets me up.'

'You can't run before you can walk, Nigel,' Belinda encouraged. 'Anything really worthwhile in life can only be achieved by application, patience, and perseverance.'

'The code of the Purcells?' He was only part-joking.

'You could say that.' Belinda glanced at him, smiling, but nervous, not sure what was coming next. Not accustomed to banter.

'And,' he asked, almost equally nervous, 'I suppose it goes for personal relationships, too?'

'Especially personal relationships,' she said firmly.

'Look, Belinda,' he asked, 'am I wasting my time with you?'

'No,' came the reply. 'I told you, brush up on your sight reading and you should sail through Grade One.'

'You know I don't mean that,' he protested.

'All right.' Belinda rose to her feet, feeling a need to put distance between them as she put her feelings into words. 'You're not wasting your time, so long as you have lots of time to waste.'

Nigel was encouraged. He grinned, 'Is that yours or is it Bob Dylan's?'

'As far as I know, it's original.' Her own words had made Belinda awkward: she took refuge in the familiar. 'Now I want you to prepare the scales of G, F and D.'

'Sod the scales!' Thwarted.

'Nigel!' Offended.

'Look,' he placated, 'You fancy going out for some chow tonight?'

'I'm sorry?' Confused, Belinda smiled politely. 'Isn't a chow some kind of dog?'

'That as well,' Nigel conceded. 'But what I had in mind was dinner.'

'Oh!' It was the first invitation to anything remotely like a date Belinda had received in longer than she cared to remember. 'Tonight?'

'Course, I realize it's a bit short notice.' Nigel hoped she was going to agree. 'What with Daddy being so doddery.'

'As a matter of fact,' said Belinda, 'he's actually in quite rude health.'

'I knew about the rude,' grinned Nigel. 'So it's okay for this evening, is it?'

'That depends.' Warily.

'What on?' Hopefully.

'Why do you want to take me out for dinner?' Cautiously.

'Why?' Confused. 'A man's got to eat.'

'And what do you expect of me?'

'What do you mean?'

'In return for dinner.'

'Belinda,' he protested, 'I'm not like that.'

'Why not?' Did she sound disappointed?

'Because you're not like that.' Nigel found it difficult to reach terms with her reserve. Difficult, but worth trying. Worth overcoming. 'Look, all I want to do is take you in one of my flash cars to the best restaurant in the South of England, where we can have a nice meal and a drop of vino and get to know each other a bit better. And then after the *petit fours*, I'll bring you home, peck you on the cheek and bid you goodnight. Now where's the harm in that?'

'Nigel!' Her smile was radiant; he felt pleased with himself. 'I'd never have guessed you were such an old-fashioned romantic! I'll be ready at eight.'

'At last!' He smiled, heading for the door. 'I never had this trouble with the Nolan Sisters.'

Oliver had never heard of the Nolan Sisters, but he had heard enough and what he had heard was enough to set his undefined war wound to acting up. Like Oliver, the wound had always had a propensity for drama. He retired to his bed.

'All I can say,' Belinda remarked later in the day, 'is that it's an extraordinary coincidence that you should be laid low with this mystery illness on the eve of my first date this decade.'

'Shame on you, Belle, to accuse me of malingering.' Oliver's voice was plaintive, his face radiating a dolour suitable to a man struggling with pain. 'Simply overdid it, that's all. If I have a fault, I suppose it's an unwillingness to admit that I, too, am subject to the inexorable passage of time.'

It was, he thought, rather a fine speech, deserving of a more sympathetic response than, 'There's nothing wrong with your tongue, is there?'

'It's nearly a hundred yards to the post office, Belinda. And it's uphill all the way back.'

'The incline,' retorted Belinda, 'is one in one hundred and fifty-seven. You can only detect it with a spirit level.'

'I wish my spirits were level.' Oliver allowed his voice to drop, fading, he hoped, with a brave wistfulness. 'I feel so giddy and weak.'

'Right.' Briskly. 'I will call the doctor.'

Oliver's voice grew stronger as he protested. 'Dr Rutherford is an incompetent quack. And there is no cure for growing old.'

'It's uncanny,' remarked Belinda, showing no sympathy but a great deal of suspicion, 'how these attacks only occur when a man enters my life. I recall you were stricken just after Simon Bishop asked me to go on a boating holiday in the Lake District.'

'And I thank heaven you didn't go,' said Oliver, fervently. 'Those lakes simply aren't safe.'

'What on earth do you mean?' gasped Belinda, wondering what tack her father was on now.

'Look what happened to poor Donald Campbell,' said Oliver in a self-satisfied tone.

'You're incorrigible!' Belinda stared at her father, torn yet again between amusement and exasperation, but still determined. 'Well, this time I'm not going to give in. It's not as if Nigel's asked me to fly to Honolulu with him.'

'Heaven forbid!' said Oliver.

'I'll only be away a few hours,' said his daughter.

'Very well.' Resigned. 'The last thing I wish to do is to spoil your evening.' Nobly. 'If anything should happen to me while you're enjoying dinner, my Last Will and Testament is in the chiffoniere.'

'Dammit!' Belinda stamped a foot. 'Is there nothing you won't say to try and get your way?'

'I know sometimes it's not easy for you, my dear.' Oliver's voice was piteous. 'But I probably shan't be here very much longer.'

'Don't make promises you don't intend to keep.'

It sounded dangerously as though she meant it, and Oliver's shocked reaction was almost sincere: 'Belinda!'

'All right.' Belinda recognized the inevitable when she saw it, and decided to give in. 'I shan't go out.'

'It's all for the best, Belle.' Oliver's voice was suddenly stronger. 'That singer chappy isn't really P. L. U.'

'Sorry?' Belinda was lost.

'People like us,' supplied Oliver; smugly.

And was horrified to hear Belinda say, 'I'll invite Nigel to have dinner with me here instead.'

'But . . . but . . .' For once Oliver was at a momentary loss for words. 'He'll be used to eating fancy foreign food at fancy foreign restaurants. What can you offer him?'

'Besides my body, you mean?'

'Belinda!' The shock was genuine now.

'Well, there's the boeuf bourguignon I was making as a special dinner for you.'

Oliver saw his victory collapse about him, betrayed by his own daughter! 'You'd give that snake *my* dinner?' he gasped.

'Someone has to eat it,' smiled Belinda, enjoying the heady taste of liberation, 'and you're far too ill for red meat.'

With which she left the bedroom and Oliver to his own bitter contemplation of defeat and a future that appeared to carry the alarming threat of disobedience in the ranks of his own household. He looked about him for inspiration, but all he could see was change and decay.

As Nigel emerged from the Grange, clad formally in a white dinner jacket with blue jeans and a satin cowboy shirt bought in New York, to eeny-meeny-miny-mo his cars, the process of selecting the Rolls for the evening, Belinda entered Oliver's bedroom bearing a tray that held a cup of tea, a bowl of tapioca, some thiny sliced bread that was lightly buttered, and a pink rose in a small vase.

'Vile muck!' winced Oliver as the tray was set across his semi-supine form.

'If you're not feeling up to it,' said Belinda with exaggerated solicitude as she moved to remove the tray.

'No, leave it.' Oliver's hands fastened on the object of

potential removal with surprising strength for one so fatigued. 'I'll try to force down a mouthful.' He paused, sniffing the air. 'Something smells appetizing downstairs.'

Belinda heard the anticipation in his voice and said unconsolingly, 'That would be the boeuf bourguignon. I put some wine in it.'

'Wine?' Oliver was aghast.

'Don't worry, I didn't raid your cellar,' Belinda soothed, 'Your bottle's safe. This is just a little *vin ordinaire* from the village.'

'I should think,' remarked Oliver acidly, 'he's used to something a little better than *vin ordinaire*.'

'Probably,' agreed Belinda casually, 'but that was all I could afford. Now, I must whip the double cream for the trifle.'

'Double . . .' Oliver's voice was hushed with longing. 'Don't go, Belle.'

It sounded plaintive enough that Belinda paused in the doorway, turning back.

'He'll be here any minute.'

But there was a note of hesitation in her voice, and Oliver heard it with an accuracy akin to the sensory capabilities of a shark. His voice was slightly hesitant as he said, 'There's something I want to say. In point of fact, I want to apologize.'

'*You?*' There was genuine amazement in Belinda's voice. 'You never apologize. Al Capone apologized more than you.'

'I realize I have prevented you from being taken to a fine restaurant . . .' Oliver let his voice tail off sorrowfully; become strong again as he announced, 'Look, damn the expense! I give you permission to open my 1970 Chateau Cantenac. Do you think you can find it?'

'Yes, Daddy.' Belinda blinked in surprise. 'There's only the one.'

'Get on with it, then.' Oliver became brusque: a man embarrassed by his own largesse. But could not resist a hint of ham: 'There's little enough time left for it to breathe. Like me.'

'Don't be maudlin.' Belinda was not sure how to take this abrupt turn of events.

'May as well try to make a decent impression,' Oliver declared gruffly. 'Assuming the lout knows the difference between claret and cherryade.'

'Sometimes you're almost human,' murmured Belinda, touched enough to cross the room and kiss her father on the forehead. 'Now eat your tapioca all up, and I may save you some trifle.'

As Belinda bustled out of the room they were both smiling, though for different reasons. Oliver spooned his tapioca with one ear cocked for the doorbell; Belinda returned to the kitchen, where she proceeded to whip the mentioned cream and then to decant the precious claret, which she was doing when the awaited doorbell rang.

'Hello, teacher,' said Nigel, extending a hand holding a bottle. 'I brought you a drop of Mouton Rothschild.'

Belinda took the offering and looked in awe at the label.

'1961!'

'Including V.A.T.'

'No,' Belinda smiled, feeling as awkward as Nigel, who was wondering why he did. 'I mean it's a very good year.'

'I'm enjoying it so far,' Nigel agreed, looking straight at her.

'The thing is,' said a slightly flustered Belinda, 'I've just decanted a bottle of Daddy's claret.'

'No sweat,' said Nigel easily, 'We'll drink that first while this one catches its breath.'

'I had better warn you,' remarked Belinda as she led the way through to the drawing room, 'that red wine goes straight to my head.'

'Best place for it,' grinned Nigel, doing his best to stay relaxed in the unfamiliar situation. 'Dad any better?'

'I suspect he'll pull through,' she replied.

'Pleased to hear it.' What Nigel wanted to hear was that Oliver would stay out of the way. 'Something smells tasty.'

'Boeuf bourguignon.'

'Really?' He bent his head to sniff her neck, 'Could have sworn it was Chanel Number Five.'

Belinda sidestepped, putting distance between them again as she asked, 'Would you like a sherry before dinner?'

'I'll stick with the wine.'

Nigel made no further move towards her as she filled two glasses and proceeded to serve an excellent dinner, pausing as she set the appetizing bourguignon on the table to ask worriedly, 'I forgot to ask you, though it's a little late now, is there anything you don't eat?'

'How do you mean?' he countered.

'One reads how you trendsetters go in for health foods . . .'

'Oh,' Nigel grinned, 'you mean the old brown rice, bean curd kick?'

'Sort of,' Belinda agreed.

'Never touch the stuff.' Nigel was emphatic. 'What I like is red meat, and lots of it.'

'That is a relief.' Belinda relaxed.

Nigel did his best to help her: 'Course, it's all a reaction to my impoverished working class background. The old tower block syndrome. Meat was a treat in them days. Mind you, my Mum wasn't the greatest of cooks. It was only when I left home that I found out beans didn't have to be orange.'

Belinda laughed and they touched glasses in a toast. It was the first of several, Oliver's prized bottle of Chateau Cantenac disappearing to be replaced in the decanter by Nigel's Mouton Rothschild. By the time the level in the decanter was closer to the bottom than to the neck, Belinda was considerably more relaxed and Nigel was feeling both well-fed and mellow. 'That was ace,' he complimented, raising a hand in mimicry of a schoolboy addressing his teacher. 'Please, Miss, can I leave the table?'

'Wouldn't you like some more trifle?' asked his hostess. 'Or can I press you to a little jelly?'

'I'd love to.' Nigel smiled at the unintentional innuendo. 'But I shouldn't have had seconds of the burfborg . . . stew as it was. Your Mum teach you to cook?'

He rose as he spoke, going over to occupy one of the armchairs set facing the fireplace. Belinda took the other, the unaccustomed quantity of wine rendering her simultaneously thoughtful and at ease.

'I suppose so,' she said. 'It seems such a long time ago.'

'So after she went, the old boy whipped you out of the Royal Academy to be his skivvy?'

'I wouldn't put it quite like that myself,' she murmured, knowing, with the clarity imparted by the wine, that there was more truth in the statement than she cared to admit.

'Don't you ever feel trapped?' he asked.

'Every day.' Belinda stared down at her glass: *in vino veritas*. 'But I love my father and I feel it's my duty.'

'He's a lucky old bugger,' remarked Nigel. 'Do you reckon he appreciates you?'

'When it suits him.' Belinda sounded wistful.

'He must rate you,' commented Nigel. 'otherwise he wouldn't go out of his way to cock up your love life.'

There was truth in Nigel, too, and Belinda was not certain she was yet ready to hear it. Assuming a cheerful defence, she said, 'If Daddy was trying to sabotage my social life, he wouldn't have let me decant his last bottle of claret.'

'But he made sure I couldn't take you out of range, didn't he?' Nigel pointed out. 'And what about the time he put the mockers on the Lake District holiday you were planning with that bloke from the Trustee Savings Bank?'

'Where did you hear that?' asked Belinda, shocked.

'You told me,' Nigel reminded her. 'Half an hour ago.'

'I did?' Belinda frowned prettily, feeling the effects of the two bottles. 'Must be the wine. It always loosens my tongue.'

'Really?' Nigel leant forwards.

Belinda said quickly, 'And there was sherry in the trifle.'

'You little devil!' Nigel smiled at her, gently mocking. 'You really know how to let your hair down, don't you?'

'No, I don't,' said Belinda with complete, if somewhat alcoholic seriousness. 'My hair has been up for longer than I care to remember.'

She sipped more claret, her face thoughtful as she studied Nigel. Then: 'No one could describe you as classically handsome, could they?'

'I don't know.' He leant back. 'I got a centre spread in Fab 208.'

'But you're quite attractive from certain angles.' The blonde head tilted attractively as she sought the certain angles. 'Hardly up to Cliff Richard standard, but . . .'

'Cliff Richard?' Nigel aped outrage. 'You trying to get off with me? I think I ought to warn you that I do like you, but I never let them kiss me on the first date.'

'Do you think I'm attractive?'

There was no banter in her tone, and Nigel answered seriously, 'Of course.'

'Oh,' Belinda backed nervously from the sincerity, 'so you like headscarves, green wellies, and thermal underwear?'

'It's nice to meet a girl with standards,' answered Nigel, feeling encouraged. 'Here, remember that exercise I liked?'

'The Mendelssohn?'

'That's the dude,' he nodded, rising. 'Though he'll have to change his name to get on 'Top Of The Pops'. Anyway, I've been working on it. If you'd care to accompany me to the keyboard?'

He held out his hand and after a moment's hesitation, Belinda took it and let him lead her over to the piano.

It was a major breakthrough of some sort, though neither of them knew exactly what sort because they were both treading unfamiliar ground.

Oliver, however, was not. He was not treading any ground because he was stretched full-length on his bedroom floor, one ear pressed to the base of any empty water glass that in turn was pressed to the polished boards of his floor, thus providing a sound conductor of sufficient efficiency that he was able to hear most of the conversation in the room below him.

'The blackguard's smoother than I gave him credit for,' he murmured as the notes of the piano joined Nigel's voice in assault on Oliver's bastion of privilege and prejudice.

'Oh, I know I've been wearing my heart on my sleeve,' sang Nigel,

'But dreams are worth sharing with someone you believe in,
And if love tastes so fine, well then why love in haste?

You're not wasting time if the time is yours to waste.
Killing time is what we say
When we have time that needs filling.
Killing time is not the way,
Time is for living, not killing.
If you're willing
Maybe we can discover how two worlds combine
When a friend becomes a lover
In the space of wasted time.'

The tune was based on the motif Belinda had demonstrated, cleverly utilized by Nigel to create a song that she found enchanting, falling almost into a reverie that was broken by the ending as the sound tailed away.

'That's as far as I've got,' he said.

Belinda smiled drowsily. 'Oh, I rather hoped you'd go a little farther. I don't wear green wellingtons and thermal underwear all the time. Oh goodness!' She broke off, reddening with embarrassment. 'That's not what I expected to say.'

'You're nice when you're pissed,' Nigel grinned.

'Do you know that I haven't been kissed by a man of below pensionable age since 1977?' asked Belinda with a sincerity that was only in part due to the alcohol. 'And that was the vicar after the Jubilee choral service.'

'What about your Dad?' asked Nigel.

'Daddy will probably be asleep by now.'

Their faces were very close together and coming closer. Belinda closed her eyes in anticipation. And Oliver entered the room on carefully-timed cue.

'Hope I'm not interrupting anything,' he remarked bluffly, 'but I'm feeling a great deal better, and I particularly want to see 'One Man and His Dog'. It's the regional semi-finals. And talking of dogs, Belle, I don't suppose there are any scraps left, are there? I'm starved.'

By the end of the last sentence he was cheerfully settled in one of the armchairs with the television switched on and the moment suitably ruined. Belinda's reply was frosty: 'I'll go and check the dustbin.'

An hour later, Oliver was happily watching the closing stages of the sheepdog trials with a thoroughly frustrated Nigel while Belinda lounged, seemingly asleep, in her chair. 'Well done, sir,' he applauded as the last sheep were penned. 'Marvellous animal, the Border Collie.'

'Prefer Brussels sprouts myself,' muttered a disconsolate rock star.

'Best programme on television in my opinion,' offered Oliver. 'A little more wine, Mr Cochrane?'

'No.' Nigel shook his head. 'I've got to drive.'

'Commendable sense of social responsibility,' applauded Oliver. 'Claret is the greatest of all wines. Rich and subtle, but strong. Belinda, would you like the last mouthful?'

He turned to his daughter and found it difficult to conceal his delight at her apparently slumbrous condition. His tone was genial and sententious as he turned back to Nigel.

'Strange how wine affects people so differently. Women especially. You're a man of the world, Mr Cochrane, you must have noticed that. Some women, for example, become irresponsible and passionate after a glass or two. Others, like my daughter, invariably fall into a deep and dreamless slumber. Well, these old bones are for bed. I'm sure you can let yourself out.'

He stood up, satisfied that his stratagems had produced their intended effects. There was no chance now of this upstart pop singer working his devious wiles on the innocent Belinda. He was, as he had himself remarked, a wily old fox. And, of course, he did know best: Belle would thank him when she came to her senses.

'Good night,' said Nigel.

He watched the old man limp from the room and glanced ruefully at Belinda. Resigned, outflanked and thwarted, he, too, stood up, crossing to Belinda's chair to plant a gentle kiss on her forehead. He was not, as she had pointed out, a handsome prince, but the kiss had an effect similar to that described in the fairy tale: Belinda awoke.

'Isn't it extraordinary,' she remarked with a smile, 'You can sleep for a hundred years and still feel tight. I thought he'd never go to bed.'

'You sly old fox!' Nigel grinned his admiration. 'Now, where were we?'

He moved to kiss her.

Belinda waited for the kiss.

Oliver came back.

'I seem to have mislaid my spectacles. Oh, you're still here. Good God! Belinda! You're supposed to be unconscious.'

'I know,' Belinda answered acidly. 'Honestly, Daddy. Are there no depths you won't stoop to?'

'To which you will not stoop,' Oliver corrected automatically, feeling alarm at these continued signs of rebellion, clearly the dual influences of excessive wine and the depraved blandishments of the damned pop singer.

The damned pop singer was embarrassed. He said, 'I really think I should be making tracks. Thanks for a lovely evening,' and hurried out as Oliver sank into a chair and poured himself the final mouthful of claret and Belinda stared with a mixture of awe and anger at her father.

'I don't understand it,' said Oliver, amiably. 'I distinctly remember that the last time you drank half a bottle of red wine you were dead to the world for twenty-four hours.'

'That was when I was ten, Daddy,' Belinda said with quiet desperation.

'Ten?' Oliver remarked. 'Seems like yesterday to me. Where's my cocoa?'

3

Oliver Purcell prided himself on his ability to make decisions swiftly and without the weakness of doubt. That the majority of his decisions were based on what were, to say the least, somewhat prejudiced values redolent of a less than impartial outlook, accompanied by a purely natural bias towards self-interest, had never occurred to him. In Oliver's world values were simple, the lines clearly drawn: Oliver was always right. These attributes co-mingled to produce instantaneous action when Oliver caught sight of the figure lurking furtively about a display of Euphorbia Pulcherima in the conservatory, the action rendered simultaneously easier and more effective by the fact that Oliver was carrying a seven pound bag of moss peat. He struck the intruder vigorously upon the head, the moss peat proving its worth as a cosh as the man slumped to the ground. Swiftly, Oliver replaced the mossy bludgeon with a weapon more suited to the instillation of terror in a supine captive: a garden fork.

'Caught you red-handed, you thieving Arab!' Oliver dropped comfortably into the idioms of an earlier age. 'You muggers don't like it, do you, when you get a taste of your own medicine?'

'I must protest,' protested the mugger.

'My God!' declared Oliver in horrified tones. 'He's wearing an old Churstonian school tie! Where did you steal that, you scoundrel?'

'If you'll let me explain,' the mugger moaned, eyeing the fork with a sensible wariness.

'You stay down there where you belong, you worm,' Oliver commanded, threatening to add four prong holes to the injuries already inflicted on the unfortunate intruder.

'But Mr Purcell,' moaned the man.

'How do you know my name?' demanded his captor.

'I am an old Churstonian,' announced the mugger with considerable indignation.

Oliver stopped to peer at his victim, thus bringing the tines of the fork perilously close to the chest, the proximity prompting the mugger to endeavour to contract his torso whilst squinting down his nose without daring to move his head. It was a feat of some difficulty and it produced a beading of sweat upon the man's brow.

'Great Scott!' cried Oliver. 'It's Ridley.'

'That's right,' said the newly christened mugger.

'I remember you.' Oliver retreated far enough for Ridley to be able to climb to his feet, though with some difficulty as his eyes remained inexorably fixed on the tines of the garden fork. 'Always wetting yourself in class, weren't you, boy?'

Combined as it was with physical threat, injury and considerable loss of dignity, not to mention the discomfort of the peat that had trickled down his collar, this reference to a past propensity preferably forgotten, added to the unfortunate Ridley's discomfort.

'Piddly Ridley.' Oliver added a little more.

'If you'll just let me explain,' begged Ridley desperately.

'Knew you'd never amount to anything,' remarked Oliver, totally ignoring the recipient of his memories. 'You were an unpleasant, whingeing youth and you've turned into an unpleasant, whingeing adult.'

'Now hold on,' complained Ridley uselessly.

'Is this what you do for a living?' Oliver continued implacably. 'Break into pensioners' houses?'

'No!' cried Ridley, unpleasantly aware that he stood in imminent danger of repeating in adulthood that weakness that had, in childhood, earned him his nickname. 'I'm Headmaster of your old school.'

'Oh, this is just a sideline, is it? Keeping your hand in between bank robberies.' It took a while for Ridley's announcement to breast the spate of Oliver's flow. 'You're the what?'

'I'm the new Headmaster of Churston County High,' said Ridley.

'Really?' Oliver's approach altered as swiftly as his attack had been delivered. 'Oh, well done, Ridley. Always knew you had it in you. May I get you something? Tea? Brandy? Brace of aspirin?'

Ridley rubbed the back of his head and wriggled as more mossy peat trickled down his back. The garden fork was lowered now, but he still regarded Oliver with the wary eye of a man approaching a bull of somewhat changeable temperament. 'I was simply calling to pay my respects,' he said. 'I hardly expected to be slugged with a sack of compost.'

'It wasn't compost,' Oliver corrected mildly. 'It was rich peat.'

'That's all very well,' said Ridley. 'But . . .'

'And if you don't want to be treated like a criminal,' advised Oliver, ignoring Ridley's protests, 'you shouldn't skulk about people's conservatories.'

'I rang the front doorbell,' said Ridley, indignantly.

'I wouldn't have heard that: I was in the garden shed getting the rich peat,' said Oliver reasonably. 'Now, if you'll excuse me, I must clear up this mess. Hand me the broom. Always pleasant to renew old acquaintances, but the flower show's looming. Good day.'

He began to sweep as Ridley ignored his dismissal and stood gulping air until words emerged in vaguely coherent form.

'No, no. If you'll bear with me, sir,' he babbled, watching the broom as it occurred to him that given the necessary amount of leverage and consequent velocity, the head might well serve as an effective bludgeon, 'Mr Purcell, the reason I called was to discuss speech day with you.'

'Speech day?' Oliver asked with sudden interest.

'As you know,' nodded Ridley, 'this year marks the school's bi-centenary and we are taking the opportunity to launch an appeal for £100,000 to build and equip a new music room.'

'Most commendable,' approved Oliver.

'Thank you,' said Ridley. 'I knew you, as Churston's greatest post-war Headmaster would want to be among the first to contribute.'

'Of course,' said Oliver, regretfully rummaging in his trouser pocket to produce a twenty pence piece, 'here you are. Wish it could be more, old man, but you know how it is, living on a fixed income.'

'No, no, sir, every little helps.' Ridley took the money quickly, marking the donation in a notebook. 'Is your . . . ah . . . daughter home?'

'You know Belinda?' Oliver's tone trod a fine line between suspicion and geniality.

'I haven't had the pleasure personally,' said Ridley, 'but I have admired her organ playing in church on Sundays.'

'You're a Christian!' barked Oliver approvingly. 'One of a dwindling band. Excellent, excellent! Belinda has gone to the shops. Baker's and fishmonger's, I think.'

'Ah,' said Ridley, brightening as he grew more confident of his safety, 'Loaves and fishes?'

'Quite,' smiled Oliver, ushering the newly approved visitor into the drawing room. 'Do sit down. One needs a miracle to live on a pension these days.'

'*Mustum transit cum id tempus,*' said Ridley.

'Oh, very good,' said Oliver, rather as though commending a clever dog. 'Do sit down.'

Ridley sat. Then stood as Belinda entered the room behind a shopping basket.

'This is my daughter Belinda,' announced Oliver, effecting introductions. 'Belle, this is Piddly . . . Mr Ridley. New Head of the High School.'

'Sorry?' said Belinda, somewhat confused.

'Sam, actually,' said Ridley, somewhat embarrassed that the legend of childhood should continue to dog his heels.

'Piddly was just a nickname,' said Oliver, conversationally. 'You know what boys are.'

'Just about,' said Belinda, no more enlightened.

'Mr Ridley was hoping to meet you,' said Oliver with ominous amiability. 'What I think one would call a fan of yours.'

'Daddy!' protested Belinda, with as little effect as the earlier protests of the luckless Ridley.

'Wouldn't be surprised if the blighter asks you out,' continued Oliver with dogged persistence. 'Eh, Ridley? If he does, I'd go. You're not getting any younger and he is in pensionable employment.'

Ridley stared at his shoes. Belinda stared at her father. Oliver smiled to himself. Piddly Ridley was not, to judge by his appearance and, to Oliver's mind, cringing attitude, much of a man but he was, at least, respectable. And a Christian, though God knew there were too many godless ones about these days. And he was, by some act of God Oliver could not yet quite understand, Headmaster of the old school. All of which was in his favour. But none so much as the fact that Ridley could be used to divert Belinda from that definitely godless pop singer.

As Oliver applied his talents as matchmaker, the cause of his efforts was visiting Mr Becket's village shop with his trusty aide. Mr Becket's was one of those emporiums found in the tiniest of hamlets, supplying such staples as tobacco, magazines and sweets from one counter whilst another was wired off for the dispensation of stamps and pensions. Mr Becket was attuned to life in Churston Deckle, to the pace and needs of its inhabitants, rather than to the demands of his celebrity customers. He was, consequently, somewhat confused by Lem's request for skins.

'You know,' supplied the roadie in answer to the proprietor's enquiry, 'fag papers.'

'Certainly, sir.' *Fag* had only one meaning for Mr Becket. 'Blue, orange, or red?'

'Ain't you got any pineapple ones?' asked Lem.

'Behave yourself, Lem,' warned Nigel without looking up from his perusal of the latest copy of *The Lady*.

'All right,' shrugged Lem, 'I'll have a dozen packets of liquorice papers.'

'Right you are, sir.' Mr Becket supplied the order. 'Now what rolling tobacco would sir prefer?'

'Tobacco?' Lem sounded confused. 'No, I don't smoke.'

'But if you don't smoke . . .' Mr Becket, too, was confused.

'He sticks them together,' explained Nigel, anxious to

avoid undue speculation and its logical conclusion, 'and lines cake tins.'

'We do sell grease-proof paper,' suggested the innocent Mr Becket.

Nigel decided it was time to save embarrasing explanations and dropped a pile of magazines on the counter alongside the numerous bags of sweets purchased by Lem.

'Anything else, sir?' asked Mr Becket.

Nigel decided there was not: 'Lem. Wallet.'

Lem paid and they were on the point of leaving Mr Becket to ponder the efficacy of lining cake tins with liquorice cigarette papers when Oliver and his walking stick limped into the shop. 'Morning, Mr P.,' greeted Nigel cheerfully. 'Lovely weather for the time of day.'

'Ah, Cochrane.' Oliver's gaze encompassed his neighbour as might a gardener's noticing a slug. 'Didn't know your sort went out in the light.'

'Come on, Nige,' suggested Lem. 'This tobacconist ain't big enough for the both of us.'

Oliver stumped past them to confront Mr Becket.

'*Country Life*?'

'I'm afraid Mr Cochrane had the last one.'

'*Field*?'

'Ditto, sir.'

'Well,' snorted Oliver, disgruntled by this disruption of his routine, 'give me the blasted *Exchange & Mart*.'

'I'm afraid,' began Mr Becket.

'Cochrane again!' barked Oliver.

'On strike, sir,' explained Mr Becket.

'Oh, chief,' interrupted Nigel, untimely, 'I don't suppose you'd like to do me a favour?'

'Your instinct is correct,' Oliver confirmed.

'Fair enough,' said Nigel, 'no sweat. I just thought you

might tell Belinda that I got that video film she wanted to see. If she'd like to pop over tonight.'

'Over my dead body!' Oliver stared aghast at the bane of his life. 'I can imagine what sort of sordid picture you'd expose my daughter to.'

'It's only *Close Encounters*,' Nigel protested.

'*Close Encounters*!' Oliver pounced with blithe inaccuracy. 'I knew it! Well, I can tell you here and now that Belinda will not be cycling over to your seraglio this evening, because she will be attending a symphony concert in Dorking.'

'Wow,' remarked Lem.

'And what's more, she's going with a man!' added Oliver, transferring his glare to the magazines bundled under the roadie's arm. 'And those are mine.'

Belinda and Sam Ridley, now accepted as Headmaster of Churston High, returned from the concert before midnight. Sam Ridley was not the kind of man to keep a lady out after the witching hour, nor, sadly, the kind of man with whom many ladies would care to be out that late. Sam's dates tended to be infrequent, brief, and not repeated. He was the kind of man who worries too much about the wrong things. He was worrying now, as Belinda led him into the drawing room of the Purcell cottage saying, 'No, of course I don't mind, otherwise I wouldn't have offered.'

'As long as your father won't object,' cautioned Sam.

'Daddy's not an ogre,' said Belinda, bending the truth out of filial affection.

'He did hit me over the head,' said Sam, remembering Oliver's introduction.

'That's just his way of breaking the ice,' said Belinda cheerfully.

'Oh, really?' said Sam.

At which point the subject of their conversation materialized in pyjamas and dressing gown and an unusually approving expression.

'Hello, Daddy,' said Belinda.

'Enjoyable concert, Belle?' asked Oliver amiably.

'Good evening, sir,' said Sam nervously. 'Yes, sir. Very good, sir.'

'The strings were a little scratchy during the second movement of the Handel,' said Belinda. 'But otherwise . . .'

'Good,' said Oliver, 'good.'

'I was just about to make some coffee,' Belinda said. 'I suppose you'd like a cup?'

'No, no, no.' Oliver shook his head, smiling with unwonted geniality upon the nervous Ridley. 'I'll leave you young things to your own devices. I know you're a gentleman, Ridley.'

And still smiling archly, he exited neatly, leaving them, unusually, alone.

'Well, if you make yourself comfortable,' said a mildly perplexed Belinda, 'I'll just put the kettle on.'

'No, don't go, Belinda. I don't really want coffee.' Sam gazed at her with unnerving intensity. 'There's something I've been wanting to ask you all night . . . In the interval, and then in the wine bar and all the way back here, I've been wondering how to frame this question.'

'It's at the top of the stairs,' said Belinda. 'Second door on the right.'

'No, Belinda,' said Sam, 'I'm serious.'

'Serious about what?' His intensity, combined with her father's arch obviousness, alarmed Belinda. 'You can't possibly be about to say what I think you can't possibly be about to say? Unless . . . No, it's too ridiculous. We only met this morning.'

'Of course, that's true, but somehow I feel we already know each other well,' said Sam, now nervous for reasons other than the threat of attack with gardening implements. 'As a rule, I'm terribly shy with girls . . . women . . . ladies.' He demonstrated this fact by blushing deeply and sliding far enough forwards in his chair that his bony knees approached the floor to render his stance ominously akin to that of a proposing suitor. 'But I know you are kind and understanding, and that's why I'm going to throw myself on your mercy and come right out with it.'

Belinda stared at him in alarm. When a man she wanted to make a proposal, whatever its nature, was about to act, her father could be counted on to make an appearance. Now, she raised her eyes to the unyielding ceiling and asked silently, 'Daddy, where are you when I need you?'

Nigel played the chromatic scale with deliberate sloppiness, prompting Belinda to admonish him, 'Now come on, Nigel. You can do better than that.'

'Don't want to,' was the petulant reply.

'God! Men never grow up, do they?' Belinda was, actually, rather pleased. 'You've been sulking all morning. Don't tell me you're jealous.'

'Me?' Nigel was scornful. 'Why should I be jealous of a middle-aged wally who wears flannel trousers? Anyway, it was a rotten concert.'

'You followed me!' Belinda was delighted.

'No! No, it was a complete coincidence,' said Nigel too quickly to sound credible. 'He must be a right piece of angel cake if your Dad approves of him.'

'Sam is very sweet,' commented Belinda, enjoying herself.

'Sweet!' Nigel pulled a face. 'Yecch.'

'You know,' said Belinda innocently, 'he popped the question last night.'

'He what?' Amazement showed on Nigel's face, accompanied by righteous indignation. 'The pushy little Herbert!'

'Well,' Belinda admitted, 'not *the* question. *A* question.'

Nigel was too alarmed to bandy words. 'Look, don't fart about,' he said bluntly. 'Belinda, you mean you're considering marrying this berk?'

'That's not what he wanted,' said Belinda vaguely.

'He's got a nerve!' Nigel was genuinely outraged now. 'Trying it on.'

'You tried it on our first date,' she pointed out.

'Yeah,' Nigel agreed, 'but I'm a rock star. He's a school-master. He's supposed to set an example.'

'Calm down, Nigel,' urged a happy Belinda.

'I won't be sending my kids to his school,' threatened the disgruntled rock star.

'Sam got nothing except a cup of milky coffee,' Belinda reassured him. 'And he spilt that.'

'Then what was he after?' demanded a suspicious Nigel.

'He wanted me for your body,' said Belinda.

'Do what?' Nigel was confused.

'I would have mentioned it sooner if you hadn't been sulking,' smiled Belinda. 'Sam wants to meet you.'

'What for?' asked Nigel. 'A duel?'

'Actually, he wants to ask you a favour.'

Belinda became serious, but Nigel remained perturbed, demanding irritably, 'Then what's wrong with him phoning the house like everybody else?'

'He did,' Belinda told him. 'But Lem answered.'

'So?' frowned Nigel.

'Lem told him to go away and spend a penny,' Belinda enlarged. 'Or words to that effect.'

'He got off lightly, then,' said Nigel. 'Lem usually tells strangers to piss off.'

'Done very well for himself, in point of fact,' remarked Oliver casually as he sat with Belinda over lunch. 'Headmaster of a respectable boy's school and barely forty.'

'Why,' asked Belinda, 'did you call him Piddly?'

'Oh,' said Oliver, regretting now that he had mentioned the unfortunate nickname, 'you know how it is with nicknames.'

'Because,' continued Belinda, 'he did have to leave his seat three times during the concert.'

'Teachers have very generous pensions these days, Belinda,' Oliver commented significantly.

'I suppose it was an unfortunate choice of programme,' Belinda murmured. 'Handel's Water Music.'

'Don't expect Cochrane made any provision for his old age,' mused Oliver. 'Mindless beatnik.'

'Nigel is a millionaire, Daddy,' Belinda said mildly.

'Today, perhaps,' acknowledged Oliver sagely, 'but has he considered the perils of inflation?'

'You always taught me it was vulgar to talk about people's money,' Belinda remarked.

'It's vulgar of Cochrane to have so much,' retorted Oliver. 'You'll be seeing Ridley again soon, I hope? Agreeable young fellow. Hair off his collar.'

In Oliver's world a pension and a decent swathe of exposed skin between hair and shirt carried more weight than millions ill-gotten through what he considered an assault on the sensibilities of people too misguided to listen to anything better.

'I suppose I'll see him on speech day,' said Belinda.

'But that's not for a fortnight.' Oliver sounded disappointed. 'Still, I expect it must be keeping him busy, what with trying to raise all that money.'

'Absolutely, Daddy,' agreed Belinda with a certain hint of guile. 'In fact, his new music room is all he thinks about.'

'Understandable.' Oliver nodded complacently. 'It's Ridley's first year. He wants to make an impression. New broom and all that.'

'He certainly does.' Belinda's enthusiasm was tinged with mischief. 'That's why he was so eager for me to introduce him to Nigel.'

'Cochrane?' Oliver's complacency evaporated. 'What on earth would the Headmaster of Churston County High School want with that representative of the great unwashed?'

'He wants him to be guest of honour on speech day, Daddy,' said Belinda with wicked innocence. 'More coffee?'

Of what Nigel's speech was a labour, he was not sure; but that it was a labour, he was certain. He had worked on it for hours. The trouble was he could not put it to music and without music he often found himself at a loss for words. He had, however, finally succeeded in setting down several pages of notes, from which he now read to Belinda and Lem.

''Cos I decided to leave school at fifteen,' he was saying when Lem pointed out, 'You was expelled.'

'Who's making this speech?' he demanded.

'He was caught behind the bike sheds,' Lem elaborated for Belinda's sake, 'with the deputy head girl.'

'I was only oiling her chain,' protested Nigel, embarrassed.

'In the nude?' Lem asked, reasonably.

'I didn't want to get my blazer dirty,' Nigel explained. 'Look, if you're gonna heckle.'

'Go on, Nigel,' encouraged Belinda. 'We were enjoying it.'

'Right.' Nigel allowed himself to be mollified. 'Where was I?'

'Leaving school at fifteen,' chorused his audience.

'Oh, yeah.' Nigel peered at his notes, cleared his throat and continued, '. . . fifteen with no qualifications, bummed around Europe for three years, joined a rock 'n' roll band and became a millionaire by the time I was twenty-three, is no reason for you lot not to concentrate on passing your G.C.E.s.'

He paused for breath, smiling to indicate he was finished as Belinda and Lem waited for more. Lem said, 'You won't get away with that load of cobblers.'

'It's a start,' said Belinda uncertainly.

'I can't stand speaking in public,' moaned Nigel. 'I don't know why I ever listened to that piddling Sam Ridley.'

'Because it's for a good cause,' urged Belinda.

'What do you think to this jacket?' Nigel was diverted by a gold lamé number.

'And enables you to contribute something to your adopted community,' Belinda continued.

'And aggravates Belinda's old man,' added Lem, which had more effect than Belinda's words on Nigel, who nodded, 'Yeah, there is that to it,' enthusiastically.

'And you've certainly succeeded on that score,' Belinda confirmed. 'Daddy's furious. He hasn't spoken to anyone since. Not even his plants.'

'I bet it really got his goat,' Lem said thoughtfully, 'when he found out Nigel was doing the new school song.'

'Actually,' Belinda said carefully, 'I haven't quite told him yet.'

'What about this one?' asked Nigel, donning a zebra stripe jacket.

As Belinda and Lem laughed, Oliver was serious. A glass of sherry in hand, he was addressing three of Churston County High's governors, two elderly gentlemen of similar appearance and outlook as himself and a tweed-clad woman.

'Far be it from a man who relinquished his Headship so many years ago to try to dictate to the governors the manner in which young Ridley should lead the school,' he announced, 'but it has been brought to my attention that he has invited an ill-educated, ill-mannered lout as guest of honour at speech day.'

'You don't mean some sort of Left Wing politician?' croaked an aghast Col (Retd) Blethridge-Snell, the horror of the thought necessitating sustenance from his host's decanter.

'Worse!' said Oliver. 'It's – I can hardly bring myself to voice the words – our local rock and roll performer.'

'You mean Nigel Cochrane?' demanded Mrs Fortescue, her tweeds aquiver.

'Alas,' sighed Oliver, 'yes, I do.'

'How exciting!' cried Mrs Fortescue, clapping her hands. 'My grandchildren are great fans of his. He used to be in a group called Graf Spee. They have all his recordings. You know, I'm very fond of the live album.'

Oliver peered at the good woman with the icy stare of an inquisitor perceiving signs of witchcraft. 'Thank you, Mrs Fortescue,' he said in a voice that matched his look, 'but I suspect that the rest of us do not share your enthusiasm. On the contrary, we owe it to our boys to offer them a wholesome and respectable example. The speaker on speech day should be someone who has attained some academic distinction, not a semi-literate teddyboy.'

'Hear, hear,' trumpeted Blethridge-Snell.

'But if we do withdraw our invitation to Mr Cochrane,' said Mr Syde-Botham, 'who can we find to replace him at such short notice?'

'Well,' murmured Oliver modestly, 'far be it from me to push myself forward, but I like to think I'm not without a certain verbal facility.'

'Yes,' agreed Mrs Fortescue with a degree of acidity. 'What I think my grandchildren would call "plenty of bunny".'

'Plenty of bunny?' frowned Blethridge-Snell.

'That's a very decent offer, Mr Purcell,' said Syde-Botham.

'Mustn't let the side down,' said Oliver.

'Then are we all in agreement?' asked Blethridge-Snell, not for a moment anticipating anything else.

'No,' said Mrs Fortescue, 'no, I really must protest.'

'You're outnumbered, Mrs Fortescue,' said Blethridge-Snell with satisfaction.

'As always,' grumbled the out-voted governor. 'You know, I feel that at these meetings . . .'

'Now play fair, Barbara,' urged Syde-Botham. 'We ought to present Mr Ridley with a united front.'

'No, it's quite all right, gentlemen,' said Oliver with practised dignity. 'We should not fear the voice of dissent. After all, tolerance is the greatest of all virtues. As I shall point out in my speech.'

Mrs Fortescue scowled at him. Syde-Botham allowed Blethridge-Snell to refill his glass. Oliver basked in their approbation, too contented with the success of his machinations to begrudge them his sherry. He was still mellowed when they left and he sat down at the chiffonière to begin drafting his speech, speaking, as usual, aloud.

'Hold the line for our most cherished traditions. No: principles . . . Tend the traditions that made this school great . . . Uphold the virtues of hard work and self-reliance . . . As Doctor Johnson said . . .'

'Talking to oneself is the first sign of insanity,' remarked Belinda as she entered the drawing room.

'Ah, Belle.' Oliver glanced round. 'Did Johnson really say that?'

'No,' said Belinda, 'I just said it about you.'

'I wasn't talking to myself,' said Oliver smugly, 'simply rolling one or two choice phrases around the palate like fine wine.'

'Daddy,' said Belinda, 'I think we should discuss speech day.'

'I will not flinch from my opposition to Cochrane, Belle,' warned Oliver. 'In fact, I've had a little pow-wow.'

'Yes.' Belinda studied the empty glasses. 'I can see you've had company.'

'Some of the school governors happened by,' murmured Oliver.

'How fortuitous,' commented Belinda.

'A little sherry, Belinda?' asked Oliver, sensing impending friction.

'Oh, thank you, Daddy,' Belinda accepted with tart politeness.

'And they were as appalled as I to learn Ridley had invited your hoodlum friend to give out the prizes,' Oliver went on as he poured his daughter a drink. 'It wasn't difficult to persuade them that he is not the sort of example we wish to set our boys.'

'I see,' said Belinda with a certain frostiness.

'Of course,' Oliver added, 'there was the little problem of finding a replacement.'

'You!' Belinda had to smile at his sheer conceit.

'Needs must,' murmured a totally unashamed Oliver. 'Noblesse oblige, etcetera, etcetera.'

'I'm sure you'll do very well,' Belinda said thoughtfully.

'Thank you, Belle,' nodded her father, assuming a victory and gratified that his daughter should accept it so graciously. 'You know, Ridley's quite well-meaning, and in the fullness of time he may make more than an adequate Head. I certainly wouldn't condemn a man for a congenital weakness of the bladder, but he's not local. He doesn't understand how deeply heartfelt are our traditions. Just because we don't go on about them . . .'

He was blithely unaware of Belinda murmuring, 'Of course we don't,' as he continued, 'It doesn't mean we shan't fight to preserve them. And if Cochrane thinks he can take over our little town, he's in for a big surprise.'

He felt it was rather a fine little speech and applauded himself afterwards with a sip of sherry, oblivious of the duality of Belinda's reply.

'I'm sure we all are, Daddy,' she said with a smile that was not, had Oliver not been gazing into the rosy glow of self-congratulation and thus seen it, reassuring to his self-satisfaction.

Speech day arrived to find Oliver's address fined and lengthened, with an emphasis on the latter. Belinda was already at the school, accompanied, unbeknownst to Oliver, by Nigel and Lem, who, as Oliver set the final touches to his speech, was testing a microphone.

'One-two,' he breathed, 'One-two.'

'I see Maths 'O' level is not de rigeur in Lem's line of business,' remarked Belinda.

‘I’ve heard him go up to four,’ said Nigel as his roadie disappeared off-stage and a worried-looking man approached them.

‘Sorry to trouble you, Mr Cochrane,’ said Herbert Packer, Churston High’s music teacher, ‘but might I have a word about this music?’

‘Belinda’s in charge of the dots,’ Nigel informed him.

‘I transcribed the music,’ Belinda expanded. ‘Is there some problem?’

‘I’m not sure.’ Mr Packer frowned, peering at the annotated sheets. ‘It’s your direction at the top of the sheet. We all understand what is meant by *andante* or *allegro non troppo*, but what exactly is meant by *reggie*?’

‘No, squire,’ Nigel said pityingly, ‘that’s reggae.’

‘I’m afraid I’m none the wiser,’ admitted Mr Packer.

‘I’ll show you,’ smiled Belinda, leading the music master away to the upright piano set to one side of the stage as Sam Ridley, dressed for the day in full regalia, strode into view.

‘Is that a mortar board?’ asked Nigel innocently, gesturing at the ceremonial headgear.

‘Yes,’ said Sam. ‘Why do you ask?’

‘My Dad had one of them.’

Sam was impressed: ‘Was he a teacher?’

‘No,’ murmured Nigel. ‘A bricklayer.’

‘Quite so.’ Sam laughed politely, not sure just how to take his celebrity guest. ‘Would you care for a spot of school luncheon?’

‘What’s on the me and you?’ Nigel asked cautiously.

‘Sausage toad, creamed potatoes and cabbage,’ Sam replied.

‘You shouldn’t have put yourself out.’

‘We like to do something special for speech day.’

Sam waited expectantly, but Nigel shook his head: ‘No,

I had a vitamin capsule before I came out. I could do with a cup of Rosie, though.' When Sam frowned incomprehendingly, he explained, 'Tea.'

'Of course.' Sam swung importantly towards a passing schoolboy. 'Mortimer! Pot of tea, on the double.'

Mortimer gaped, wondering what Piddly Ridley was going on about. 'Where from, sir?' he asked.

'Don't take that attitude with me, laddie. Go to my office and speak to Miss Spurway. Now cut along.' Sam smiled to himself at this firm display of authority until he saw young Mortimer ogling Belinda's legs, an observation delayed by his own perusal. He shouted at the boy again, then smiled at Nigel, 'I'll let you get on, Mr Cochrane. And I'd like to say what an honour it is for us to have you here today.'

'Yeah, I suppose it must be,' admitted Nigel.

'And you're sure you don't mind Mr Purcell supplanting you as main speaker?' worried Sam.

'No,' assured Nigel, 'To be truthful, it was a weight off my mind. Lets me concentrate on what I do best.'

Several hours later he was waiting to do what he did best as Oliver did his. The speech was seemingly interminable, the ranks of youngsters facing the stage fidgeting beneath the glazed gazes of the governors, their spouses, the teachers, the prefects, Belinda and Nigel. Lem might have gazed out, too, but he had already fallen asleep as Oliver intoned, 'And so, having looked back at the last two hundred years . . .'

'Which is about how long he's been talking,' whispered Nigel.

'We must always hold in the forefront of our minds the truth that it is upon the foundation of our traditions that we build for the centuries ahead, for in a changing, tawdry world we must remain steadfast and sturdy.'

Oliver gazed sternly over the blank faces as he gathered

up his notes and the dignitaries on the stage woke up to the fact that he had, at last, finished. There was a moment's relieved silence, then a burst of polite applause as Sam Ridley rose to take the lectern and Nigel slipped quietly to the rear of the stage.

'On behalf of the school,' said Sam, 'its parents and old boys, I would like to thank Mr Purcell for his stirring address. And now we will all stand for the singing of the school song.'

At the rear of the stage, curtains swung back to reveal Nigel standing at the microphone before the augmented ranks of the choir as Oliver burst into hearty, if somewhat tuneless, voice with 'Yeoman Of Churston'.

'No, Mr Purcell,' muttered an embarrassed Sam Ridley, tugging at Oliver's sleeve. 'The *new* school song.'

'New?' barked Oliver, staring at Ridley as if recognizing signs of incipient madness. 'What are you blithering on about, Piddly?'

Sam moved back as though from a snarling dog and Oliver was left alone at the centre of the stage as Nigel led the boys in a reggae-rhythmed song he had called 'Brother'. For a long moment, Oliver stared in rage and horror as the audience joined in enthusiastically, then he stepped to the side, glowering at the song sheet Belinda, like everyone in the hall except him, held.

'What the hell has been going on?' he demanded furiously.

'I would have thought that was patently obvious by now,' Belinda retorted.

'How dare he?' Oliver stared balefully at Sam. 'The jumped-up Barnsley bed-wetter! My poor school.'

And with that he stumped from the stage, never a man to accept defeat gracefully.

* * *

'Daddy! Daddy!' Belinda hurried into the cottage, alarmed at her father's reaction to the thwarting of his plans for Nigel's humiliation. 'Oh, there you are.'

In the conservatory Oliver refused to turn his head from the plant he was furiously tending as he said bitterly, 'If the object of the exercise was to humiliate me in front of 650 people, then your plan succeeded admirably.'

Belinda sighed, realizing that his hurt was real and seeking to placate him. 'I'm sure that was the last thing Sam Ridley intended.'

'Ridley? He's just a cat's paw,' snapped Oliver, propelling his wheelchair vigorously across the room. 'Cochrane's the Svengali behind it all. And you're in his thrall. He's turned you against your own father!'

'That's nonsense,' Belinda said reasonably. 'Nigel did the school a great favour.'

'A favour?' snorted Oliver. 'Call that tuneless cacophany a favour?'

'Several of the staff were seen to tap their feet,' protested Belinda.

'Lily livered turncoats to a man!' Oliver scoffed.

'At least you can understand why I never told you about the new song,' said Belinda. 'I knew you'd get yourself into a distemper.'

'And isn't my anger justified?' complained Oliver. 'The old school song was perfectly serviceable.'

'But it wasn't commercial, Daddy,' Belinda told him.

'It's a school song, not a brand of dog food!' barked Oliver. 'Give me a single justification for overturning two centuries of tradition.'

'The music room appeal,' said Belinda. 'Your twenty pence will hardly pay for a glokenspiel hammer. You see, Nigel's bringing the new school song out as a record.'

'That puerile jingle!' Entrenched in his own concepts of

taste and propriety, Oliver found this hard to understand; harder still to accept that he was roundly trounced by Nigel.

'And he's donating all the proceeds to the appeal fund,' continued Belinda. 'If it's a hit, your old school will make thousands.'

Oliver sank deeper in his wheelchair and asked grumpily, 'I suppose he'll want to be a school governor.'

Belinda saw that the real anger had passed and smiled as she shook her head and said, 'Oh no, Daddy.'

'Why not?' demanded Oliver, surprised.

'They've already asked him,' said Belinda. 'He turned it down. Shall I make some tea?'

4

Oliver, as Sam Ridley's visit had demonstrated, was not accustomed to finding strangers in his conservatory, so when a voice that was both female and American asked, 'Pardon me, but do you speak English?' he was immediately both put out and on his guard.

'Of course I speak English!' he snapped. 'It's my mother tongue.'

Despite feeling somewhat insulted, he opened the door to the woman, perceiving that she was young, dressed in furs and jeans, and, he supposed, pretty. 'Far out!' she said. 'Where I come from all the gardeners are Mexican.'

Obviously she was foreign and therefore to be treated with the tolerance reserved for lesser species, but even so Oliver found it difficult to keep his temper in the face of this outrageous aspersion. 'I'm not the gardener,' he announced with frosty dignity. 'This is my house.'

'Really?' The strange woman looked around, wandering casually into the drawing room where she proceeded to study the knick-knacks as though appraising them for possible purchase and thus infuriating Oliver further. 'It's so cute. Is it for sale?'

'Certainly not!' bellowed Oliver.

'Oh, too bad. I really love all these tiny little English cottages.' She smiled radiantly at the apoplectic Oliver. 'Tell me, do you know the way to the Grange?'

He might have known it! Certainly, he had forecast it: let that damned pop singer take over the Grange and before anyone knew it, Churston Deckle would be overrun by people who were definitely not like us. But politeness at all times. He asked, 'Are you walking, or did you come by car?'

'Oh,' said the invader, 'I have a cab waiting.'

'Certainly,' said Oliver with exaggerated patience. 'You go out of this door, down the path, straight up the lane and it's in front of you. But it isn't for sale either, unfortunately. Some damn' pop singer lives there.'

'I know all about Nigel Cochrane,' said the woman knowingly.

'Oh?' Oliver felt interest stir. 'What are you? Some sort of autograph hunter?'

'You could say that, honey,' said the woman. 'I'd just love Nigel's autograph. On a blank cheque.'

As the mysterious visitor prepared to descend upon the Grange, Lem was preparing to do something about the squalor that existed within the elegant building. As he was the first to point out, Lem was accustomed to room service and Nigel was accustomed to having Lem around to call room service for him, so relatively little housework had been done since they took up residence. The net result was devastation upon which Belinda had remarked, the plaintive response prompting her to recommend Mrs Tibbs, a local woman known to ply a duster in return for financial consideration. This good woman was now eyeing with some apprehension the results of some weeks' occupation by two men accustomed to room service.

'That's it,' Lem was telling her. 'As I said before, it's not really that hard a place to keep clean.'

'It's a lot muckier than the vicarage,' commented Mrs Tibbs professionally.

'All right.' Lem knew the opening of a haggling session when he heard it. 'One pound twenty-five.'

'Two,' said Mrs Tibbs firmly.

'One fifty,' countered Lem.

'Two.' Mrs Tibbs held her price. Looking around, she felt she had the upper hand.

'One seventy-five,' said Lem. 'And that's it.'

'Done!' said Mrs Tibbs.

'Well and truly,' said Lem as Nigel wandered into the room wearing only a gold chain and a cashmere dressing gown. 'Oh, Nige.'

'He looks older than I expected.' Mrs Tibbs studied Nigel with a clinical eye that appeared not at all impressed by what it saw. 'I've never been this close to a legend before. More care-worn.'

'You're seeing him at a bad time of day,' Lem told her. 'During the hours of daylight.'

Nigel peered blearily at the pinafored Mrs Tibbs and beckoned Lem over. 'Lem,' he said, 'A word in your shell-like. She's a bit old for you, ain't she?'

'No, this ain't a pull,' assured Lem. 'It's Mrs T., the cleaning lady.'

'Cleaning lady,' murmured Nigel, grasping the idea slowly. 'Welcome aboard, Mrs T.'

Mrs Tibbs smiled graciously and informed him, 'My Pauline's little Darren is a big fan of yours.'

'Pleased to hear it,' said Nigel.

'I don't see it myself,' Mrs Tibbs went on. 'Course, they're never the same in the flesh, are they?'

'No,' Nigel agreed.

'I don't mean to pry,' pried Mrs Tibbs, 'but aren't you friendly with Mr Purcell's Belinda?'

Nigel began to get the look he had been getting lately when anyone mentioned Belinda. It was a composite of embarrassment, irritation and confusion. Lem said quickly, 'Yeah, that's right.'

'Shame really, isn't it?' queried an expansive Mrs Tibbs, feeling, now that business was completed and a price agreed, that she was at home. 'Pretty girl like that wasting her life on a man who doesn't appreciate her.'

'Nige does appreciate her,' said Lem defensively. 'Given half a chance, he could appreciate her a lot. Know what I mean?'

'I meant Mr Purcell,' said Mrs Tibbs. 'Not that we don't all respect him, the miserable old soldier.'

'You're right there, love,' agreed Lem, sincerely.

'Yes,' agreed Mrs Tibbs.

'Listen,' Lem said with a conspiratorial air, 'I'll tell you something . . .'

'All right, Lem,' warned Nigel, 'enough is enough.'

'Of course,' said an unperturbed Mrs Tibbs, 'you celebrities can have any woman you take a fancy to.'

'You don't want to believe everything you read in the *T.V. Times*, love,' Nigel disagreed. 'I lead a very quiet life. We don't have women up here, do we, Lem?'

'No,' Lem said sadly, 'we don't.'

'Except my piano teacher and your good self,' said Nigel, settling into an armchair as the door behind him opened and the dark-haired woman who had examined Oliver's cottage tip-toed into the room. 'It's quite a monastic existence.'

In the eyes of Mrs Tibbs this statement was questionable in view of the sudden appearance of a woman who wore what Oliver Purcell would describe as rouge and pancake and who draped herself about Nigel's person as both hands slid inside his dressing gown to a cry of, 'Guess who? Hi, Nige,' rising to apparent delight with,

'Nigel! You're in the buff! You must have known I was coming.'

Mrs Tibbs stared transfixed, memorizing every detail for future reference as Nigel's mouth opened and an expression of horror transfixed him in turn.

'Oh, God! An endless queue,' groaned Oliver as he studied the handful of pensioners lined before the window of Mr Becket's post office counter.

'Will you be all right if I pop across to the baker's?' asked Belinda solicitously.

'Of course,' snapped an irritable Oliver, 'I'll be all right. I'm not a child.'

'Delightful morning, eh, sir?' said an innocent Mr Becket.

'When I want your opinion, Becket, I'll ask for it,' growled Oliver.

'Daddy!' Belinda reprimanded, explaining to the newsagent, 'His leg's playing up.'

'There's no need to tell everyone,' Oliver snarled. 'Get a move on, girl, or there'll be nothing left but factory bread and yesterday's bath buns.'

'Yes, Daddy,' said Belinda meekly, choosing discretion as the better part of valour.

'And mind the traffic,' admonished Oliver as though addressing a child.

Belinda made as swift an exit as the arrival of Mrs Tibbs allowed, thankful to be rid of Oliver for a while. Since the introduction of Churston High's new school song Oliver's moods had tended to be a trifle less than sunny, the simultaneous defeats of his matchmaking and commandeering of speech day clouding his vision. The additional aggravation of his genuinely injured leg served to render comparison with a sore-headed bear unfavourable. Thus it was he was not in the most amiable frame of mind as Mrs Tibbs joined him in the queue.

'Good morning, Mr Purcell,' she said cheerily. 'Thank heavens it's pension day.'

'Although in your case, Mrs Tibbs,' said Oliver with disdain, 'no doubt your pension is merely one of a number of sources of remuneration.'

'Eh?' said Mrs Tibbs, wondering why school-masters always used long words.

'I trust you have informed the Department of Health and Social Security,' said Oliver sarcastically.

'About what?' asked Mrs Tibbs, innocently.

'The extra money you earn charring,' declared Oliver as might prosecuting counsel, producing some damning piece of evidence.

'That doesn't count,' argued Mrs Tibbs.

'Nonetheless,' Oliver said pompously, 'no doubt it is cash in hand?'

'What little there is of it,' said Mrs Tibbs pathetically. 'I only do the vicarage and now the Grange.'

'Hmph!' Oliver yielded a little: the stern, but just patriarch. 'I suppose you deserve a little extra for putting up with all that degeneracy.'

'No, no!' Mrs Tibbs shook her head vigorously. 'Those stories about Reverend Sclater-Booth are completely without foundation. And Mr Cochrane and his friend couldn't be nicer. Of course,' her voice lowered as voices do when discussing such matters as decent people do not discuss, 'they're not normal.'

'You astound me,' said Oliver ironically.

'They have different ways, these show business personalities,' continued Mrs Tibbs, taking Oliver's comment for encouragement. 'Creatures of the night! When I got there this morning they were just going to bed. They don't wear pyjamas, you know.'

This titbit was greeted with boredom. Oliver said, 'Frankly, I'm not in the least interested.'

But Mrs Tibbs held a different opinion. 'You should be,' she warned ominously, contradicting herself with, 'I'm not one to gossip, but I was up at the Grange yesterday and, well, I don't like to speak out of turn, but if your Belinda was my daughter . . .'

Oliver had much to think about as he collected his pension and laboured painfully up the one in one hundred and fifty-seven gradient to the cottage. There were, of course, Belinda's feelings to be considered, and no one could accuse him of being an insensitive man, and she had without doubt formed some odd attachment to that damned singer. Which, in fact, made his conduct all the worse. Trifling with Belle's feelings! It was a good thing she had a father who concerned himself with her best interests rather than putting himself first. And in her best interest she had to know, he decided as they entered the cottage.

'Are you sure you're all right?' asked Belinda with charming solicitude as they came into the drawing room. 'You've been abnormally quiet all the way back from the shops. If it's your leg, you should have stayed here.'

'It's not my leg,' Oliver said, 'It's just that I've had much to think about.'

'Oh dear,' sighed Belinda. 'My fault for giving you fish for dinner last night. I'll make some coffee.'

Oliver sank wearily into a chair, his expression that of a man with a sad, but unavoidable task to perform. 'No,' he said, 'sit down. There's something I have to tell you. It's very important.'

'You've fallen in love,' joked Belinda, 'and you want my permission to marry.'

'Belinda, my dear,' said Oliver in his most solemn tones, 'I take no pleasure from what I have to say, but I experienced an unpleasant revelation in the pension queue.'

'Old Mr Jessop forgot to button his fly again?' Belinda asked cheerfully.

'I'm quite serious, Belle,' Oliver murmured. 'This will come as a shock, my dear, but it's best that you know: Cochrane has had another woman up at the Grange.'

'Oh, is that all?' Belinda was unperturbed. 'I know about that. It was my idea.'

Horror overcame Oliver. He could scarcely believe the evidence of his own ears. He gasped, 'It was what?' in tones of disbelief.

'After all,' said Belinda calmly, 'there are some things you can't expect two men, living alone, to do for themselves.'

'Are my ears deceiving me?' demanded Oliver as his worst fears loomed large in his imagination. 'Are you condoning this lascivious conduct?'

'You've been listening to gossip, haven't you?' Belinda laughed.

'Yes,' Oliver admitted with all the dignity he could muster, 'but it was gossip of the highest quality.'

'You shouldn't be so suggestible,' Belinda admonished. 'The other woman in Nigel's life is Mrs Tibbs, whom I recommended to clean up their midden.'

'I know about Mrs Tibbs,' said Oliver, regret and relish mingling. 'It was she who told me about the other woman.'

'Another woman?' Belinda was suddenly serious.

'Yes,' Oliver confirmed solemnly, 'some typical American woman called Laura. I forgot to tell you. She called here – wanted to buy my house. And according to Mrs Tibbs, she and Cochrane seemed to know each other rather well.'

'Oh, Laura. Yes,' said Belinda with some relief, 'Nigel's told me all about her. She's just someone he used to go out with in America, that's all.'

Then her relief evaporated as her father faced her with a serious expression and said, 'I'm afraid that isn't all, Belle. She's Cochrane's wife.'

Nigel had, indeed, told Belinda something of Laura, whose photograph, until her arrival at the Grange, had formed an integral part of his dartboard, but not all. He had omitted certain parts that, added together, amounted to most. Amongst those aspects he preferred to forget were three important facts: he was married to Laura; Laura liked to spend his money; he was terrified of Laura. And now Laura had descended upon his rustic retreat to reduce him to a ragged bundle of indecisive nerves. The effect was not dissimilar to that of an announcement that the *Titanic* was taking on more ice: blind panic. And worse, Laura had come with a purpose.

'Don't try to bullshit me,' she warned as Nigel twitched in his luxurious living room. 'I know how you operate.'

'No, honest, Laura,' he squirmed, 'there's nothing between Belinda and me.'

'It was all in *Rolling Stone*,' Laura announced with confidence.

'You don't want to believe anything you read,' said Lem. 'We've told you already – she's old.'

'Oh yeah, right,' agreed Nigel a little too eagerly. 'Old.'

'So if it isn't her there'll be some chick else,' countered an undiverted Laura, 'somewhere in the frame. And when I find out who she is, you'll hear from my lawyers.'

'Don't tell me,' said Nigel with as much defiance as he could muster, which was not a lot, 'you can't be jealous.'

'Not jealous,' murmured Lem. 'Greedy.'

'Look, Laura,' Nigel said desperately, 'there must be some way we can work this out. Quite amicably.'

'Sure there is,' confirmed Laura with alarming enthusiasm. 'I divorce you and get half of everything you own. That's the law.'

'And to think she used to be such a young, sweet girl,' commented Lem.

'That's absolutely right,' agreed Laura, undeterred. 'Young and sweet before I left my family in Buffalo and put up with all your obsessions. I became a vegetarian! And I was living in hotel rooms, Nigel. You got the best years of my life. I gave up my career to support you, Nigel.'

'What career?' wondered Lem. 'All you ever did was shop.'

'Don't aggravate her, Lem,' pleaded the object of Laura's diatribe.

'I also advised you,' Laura continued. 'Guided your feet on the artistic pathway.'

'Fantasy Island,' murmured Lem as Nigel crouched goggle-eyed with terror.

'So I think, Nigel,' Laura suggested brightly, 'I'm entitled to the house in Santa Barbara and the place in Hawaii, or the forest in Wales and the horse ranch in Australia. I'm flexible.'

'Yeah,' said Lem. 'She's very considerate. Anything else?'

'Not at the moment,' Laura said, with what she felt was

reasonable generosity. 'Of course, my attorneys will need to audit your accounts to ensure I get my rightful due.'

'Leave it me, Nige,' Lem suggested menacingly, 'and I'll make sure she gets what's coming to her.'

'Will you tell this guy I do not get off on hostility?' asked Laura, favouring Lem with a poisonous glare.

'Half of absolutely everything,' Nigel murmured in tones stricken simultaneously with awe and panic.

'Cheer up, Nige,' Lem said bitterly, 'that still leaves you an arm and a leg.'

As Nigel considered the prospects of such financial imbalance the phone rang. Lem went to answer, but Nigel waved him back.

'Leave it, Lem. I'm not feeling sociable.'

The answering machine did its thing and at the other end of the line Belinda set the phone down with some force. Oliver's news had not left her best pleased; indeed, it had left her more than a little alarmed. Her relationship with Nigel was undefined, but so far as she was concerned it did not include the importation of other women to the Grange and while she was confident that there was nothing more to it than village gossip, the fact that the answerphone was on suggested that so might something else be. Not in the best of tempers she entered the drawing room, where Oliver was drafting yet another letter to *The Times*.

'The Editor, *The Times*, Printing House Square, etcetera, etcetera,' he murmured. 'Sir, as Virgil put it with such precision, *Agmine facto, Ignavum fucos pecus a praesepibus arcent.*'

'I didn't even get to see him,' announced Belinda, then saw that her father was engrossed in a letter. 'Writing to *The Times*?'

'Good idea,' said Oliver. 'So am I.'

'Daddy,' Belinda remarked, 'there comes a time when eccentricity spills over into clinical insanity.'

'Don't you feel well, Belle?' asked Oliver with concern.

'I'm talking about you!' Belinda's tone was unusual enough. To see her cross to the sideboard and pour herself a large brandy was more so.

'Brandy, Belinda?' queried Oliver. 'Are you upset, my dear?'

'Upset?' Belinda quaffed deep of the brimming glass. 'I'm bloody furious!'

'Language, Belinda!' Oliver reprimanded, though with genuine shock, for these were not words familiar to his daughter's vocabulary.

'I'm sorry.' Belinda shook her head and poured more brandy. 'But there are some of us who can't express all our feelings in Latin.'

'So you've had it out with Cochrane, have you?' asked Oliver with a certain degree of optimistic relish.

'We haven't had anything out. He won't even answer the telephone,' snapped Belinda, partaking of more brandy. 'All I get is some stupid message. Of course, now Laura's back in his life, he doesn't need me anymore.'

'Does she teach piano too?' asked Oliver with infuriatingly bland innocence.

'Give me strength!' Belinda pleaded. 'How could he do this to me?'

'It was best you found out what sort of man he was before you became too involved,' Oliver intoned, rather enjoying what he saw as a victory over his arch adversary. 'You can never win with his sort. Either he discards you because you won't submit to his vile demands, or he has his evil way with you and then grows bored.'

His pomposity strained the limits of Belinda's lengthy patience. 'If you're asking me if I've been to bed with him,' she declared, 'the answer is a) no, and b) it's none of your damn' business if I have!'

'Of course it's my business,' retorted Oliver in aggrieved tones. 'You're my little girl.'

'Aren't I just?' snapped the woman in question, sinking into a chair with glass and decanter in hand.

'I know it's a cliché, Belle, but there are plenty more fish in the sea,' Oliver remarked. 'And we still have each other, you and I.'

'That's not enough!' Tears choked Belinda's voice. Oliver stared at her with stern incomprehension.

'Control yourself, girl. Remember whose daughter you are.'

'How can I forget?' Belinda wailed. 'Every waking minute of every bloody day, I'm made to remember whose daughter I am! I'm nearly thirty-two . . .'

'Thirty-three,' corrected Oliver helpfully.

'But everywhere I'm still Mr Purcell's Belinda, as if I didn't exist on my own.' The brandy weakened the restraints of the years, letting the frustrations flood forwards. 'This little house and this little town are like a prison sometimes! That's why I felt so different with Nigel. He isn't hemmed in by parish boundaries, the world is his oyster. And I thought perhaps he would show me that world . . . That he saw me as an individual in my own right. At least he made me feel . . .'

She broke off and Oliver stared at her with concern replacing his stern expression. 'What did he make you feel?'

'As if I was different, special. An adult. A . . . a . . .'

'A woman, I suppose?' Oliver supplied.

'What's wrong with that?' Belinda was defensive. 'I *am* a woman. And now this Laura . . .'

'He's hurt you, hasn't he?' Oliver softened perceptibly.

'You're so perceptive,' said Belinda.

'I didn't realize Cochrane meant so much to you,' said Oliver in a wondering tone.

'Neither did I,' said Belinda.

The situation changed by this new perception of his daughter's feelings, Oliver's approach immediately changed. Family loyalties came first and he was, at heart, genuinely concerned for his daughter's happiness. 'You can't let that man cast you off like an old . . .' He sought the appropriate word. 'An old . . .'

Belinda supplied it: 'Maid?'

'Precisely,' agreed Oliver. 'You owe it to yourself to go up to the Grange.'

'I'm not crawling to him in front of her,' Belinda said sulkily.

'I should think not!' Oliver declared firmly. 'You must beard the beast in his den and teach him not to trifle with your affections.'

'How can I?' Belinda was interested. 'I probably won't even get past the guard on the gate.'

'Nonsense,' Oliver said stoutly. 'Come with me, I'll show you how to deal with the likes of him.' He shook his head sadly, 'I knew you shouldn't have given my horse whip to the W. I. Bring and Buy.'

A sudden entrant to Nigel's large living room would have been struck by two things. The first was that the place was tidy. The second, that Lem was showing signs of incipient madness as he rummaged about the room talking loudly to himself.

'You seen my fag papers?' he asked the emptiness. 'They were on the floor under that old sardine sandwich. I can't find nothing since Mrs T.'s been.'

'If they meet, the game's up.'

The voice was suitably hollow for one that came, apparently, out of thin air.

'Still a bit out of order banning Belinda like that,' replied Lem. 'It's Laura you want to send packing.'

'That's easier said than done, Lem.' Nigel's pallid, care-worn features emerged from behind the sofa, where he crouched in the lotus position, vainly seeking solace in meditation. 'She's brought fourteen pieces of luggage! You don't understand what a difficult position I'm in. She's a monster. She'd rip Belinda apart.'

At this point, Belinda and Oliver came unannounced into the room. Nigel, raw terror lending his features the attributes of jelly, rose as far as his knees. Lem said, 'How did you get in?'

'An old solider,' replied Oliver with some satisfaction, 'is not without resource.'

'Lem,' wailed Nigel, 'go down the gatehouse and sack Emil again.' He turned panic-struck eyes on Belinda. 'Look Belinda, I know all this seems . . .'

'Pretty rotten,' prompted Lem.

'The way I've been . . .' said Nigel.

'Behaving,' finished Lem.

'But I can . . .' Nigel broke off.

'He can explain,' explained Lem.

'I'm not interested in your glib explanations,' said Belinda with brandy-born briskness. 'I fell for your shallow charms once, and once is enough.'

'Hear, hear,' encouraged Oliver.

'I was foolish enough to believe you respected the fact that I didn't care to leap into your bed at the drop of a hat.'

'Steady on, girl,' warned Oliver.

'Quiet, Daddy,' ordered Belinda. 'But instead, it turns out you have Laura to fall back on – and I am choosing my words carefully – *and* she's your wife! You're still married! It's incredible. I'm lost for words! And another thing . . .'

'Hold on, hold on.' Nigel rose to his feet, if not his full height, which was difficult to reach thanks to the weight of cares on his shoulders and the stiffness of the lotus position. 'It's not like that. Is it, Lem?'

'Isn't it?' Lem looked surprised. But remained loyal: 'No. It just looks like that.'

'Looks like that,' repeated Nigel. 'You gotta try to understand, Belinda, that we're not dealing with a normal person here.'

'So he admits it!' Oliver pounced triumphantly. 'At long last!'

'I'm talking about Laura!' protested Nigel. 'Laura's a flake! A fruitcake. A nut.'

'Very nourishing, though,' murmured Lem.

'After she goes to her psychiatrist, he has to go to his psychiatrist,' continued Nigel. 'That's why I left her. 'Cos she was driving me to my psychiatrist.'

'And she's a terrible driver,' Lem threw in.

'Assuming, for the sake of argument,' said Belinda with ice in her voice and a faint stirring of hope in her heart, 'that this farrago of excuses contains a scintilla of fact.'

'Bravo!' applauded Oliver, ever one to enjoy a long-winded turn of phrase.

'She's lost me,' frowned Lem.

'Then why haven't you simply told her she is persona non grata?' finished Belinda.

'Cos he doesn't know what it means,' suggested Lem.

'It's not as simple as that,' moaned Nigel.

'You're frightened of her, aren't you?'

Belinda saw the truth. Nigel said, 'No. No, not frightened.'

'Try terrified,' Lem advised.

'How pathetic,' said Belinda contemptuously. And was about to say more, but was halted by the arrival of Laura herself, burdened under the weight of all that Churston Deckle might offer in the way of tourist knick-knacks. Belinda saw that she was rather lovely, superbly groomed, and expensively dressed, but, perhaps thanks to the brandy or perhaps thanks to her feelings for Nigel, she remained undaunted.

'Nigel,' announced the lady, 'I don't know how you can say there's nothing to buy in Churston Deckle. I've found the most darling little shop.'

'So she bought it,' commented Lem.

'It's only money, honey,' smiled Laura, setting down her acquisitions so that she saw Belinda and Oliver for the first time. 'Why didn't you tell me you had company?'

'How do you do?' Belinda stepped forward as might a Christian to a lion. 'I'm Belinda Purcell. You must be Mrs Cochrane.'

'Oh, so you're Nigel's little piano,' Laura paused carefully, 'mistress. At last! Now I know why Nigel wasn't about to introduce us. Nigel,' she said to the quaking rock star, 'she could be quite pretty. Sweetheart,' turning to Belinda with a condescending smile, 'you must let me take you to the beauty parlour.'

'How dare you, madam?' Oliver's intervention in defence of his daughter was rendered fiercer by the fact that this patronizing female was foreign. 'My daughter has no need of paints and pancake. She has the natural beauty of the English rose.'

'Nigel,' said Laura, 'I didn't know you had a gardener.'

'Madam, I keep telling you,' said a pained Oliver, 'I am not a gardener.'

'Nigel,' said Laura, ignoring him, 'you didn't do Miss Purcell justice. Sixty? She doesn't look a day over forty-five.'

'You told her I was sixty?' gasped Belinda.

'For your own good,' claimed Nigel.

'He thought it would keep Laura off your back,' expanded Lem.

'*Sixty?*' Belinda, or the brandy, was not to be assuaged. 'That is it, Mr Cochrane! Daddy, we're going! But first there's something I owe you.'

She moved towards Nigel, rummaging in her handbag. Laura, who was standing proprietorially close to Nigel, screamed, 'She's got a gun!' And dived behind the sofa.

'This isn't Dallas,' said Belinda scornfully, extracting bank notes from the bag. 'Here. For lessons paid for and not received.'

'Oh no, Belinda.' Nigel shook his head, his panic abject as he pleaded, 'Lem! Help!'

Belinda spun on her low heel and stalked towards the door, closely followed by the limping Oliver. Lem moved after them as Laura smiled in triumph and Nigel stared goggle-eyed and speechless. 'Don't go, love,' he urged sincerely. 'Give Nige a break. He needs you.'

'He needs tarring and feathering,' barked Oliver.

'No, hold on.' Lem shook his head, his face serious for once. 'It's not really his fault. He's just unfit to cope with the real world. I've always tried to shelter him.'

'Come on, Belle,' urged Oliver. But Belinda looked back and was caught by the pathetic figure that Nigel Cochrane, rock superstar, cut; and by Laura's triumphant, 'Bye, bye.'

'No, Daddy,' she said, 'I'll join you in a minute. There's something I want to ask Mrs Cochrane. Lem, show Daddy the garden.'

'Here.' Lem seized Oliver's arm before any protest could escape and hauled him through the door. 'Why don't I give you the guided tour?'

'I thought you were leaving,' said Laura tartly.

'I was about to leave, but there's something I want to know.' Belinda was cool and calm, her poise dangerous. 'Why was Nigel so desperate to prevent us meeting?'

'Isn't she innocent?' Laura asked Nigel and smiled at Belinda. 'You're worth a lot of money to me, honey. Sure, Nigel pays me an allowance, but now I can screw him for a really fat divorce settlement.'

'How sweet,' said Belinda venomously.

'Isn't it just?' agreed Laura. 'And you can co-star as the other woman.'

'I told her we hadn't,' said Nigel helplessly, 'you know . . .'

'That is neither here nor there,' Belinda dismissed him, taking matters firmly in her own hands. 'What you have to understand is that Nigel can't think straight because he's afraid of you. And you can't think straight because that is the kind of woman you are.'

'Belinda,' wailed Nigel, anticipating imminent eruption. 'Please!'

'Quiet, Nigel,' hushed Belinda, facing Laura in more ways than one, 'And for some reason you seem to assume that an English divorce court throws people's money around the way I've read they do in America.'

'That's why I couldn't afford to dump her over there,' Nigel explained mournfully.

'Whereas in reality,' continued an implacable Belinda, 'if you divorce Nigel here, you'll be lucky if they award you a one-way ticket to Gatwick, let alone alimony. Our judges don't have much time for lazy, self-indulgent, pampered, spoilt, immature trollops like you.'

Laura took this in her stride. 'All right,' she retorted, 'then you'd like to see your name splashed all over the gossip columns as Nigel's mistress?'

'No,' allowed Belinda fairly, 'but then it would be ages before the case came to court. Can you survive here for months? Especially if Nigel stops your pocket money?'

'Right!' cried a much encouraged Nigel before wilting beneath Laura's scowl.

'Nigel tells me,' said Belinda, pressing the point, 'that you're the sort of woman who suffers withdrawal symptoms if she loses her credit cards.'

'I wish I was taping this,' murmured an admiring Nigel.

'You'll get yours, Cochrane,' Laura threatened.

Belinda stepped back. She had done her best. There was no more to add except, 'It's up to you, Nigel. If you're still terrified of her . . .'

'No,' said Nigel in an awed voice, gazing at her adoringly, 'Not half as terrified as I am of you.'

The photograph of Laura was still missing from the dartboard, but Lem could imagine it was there as he tossed the arrows wishing it was tomorrow and the lady was already gone. She came into the room with a case and the announcement that Nigel's bedroom door was still locked.

'Yeah,' nodded Lem, 'he's still under sedation.'

Laura dropped her fox fur coat to glance at her Piaget. 'And I've got to get to the airport,' she said.

'You're not leaving us so soon?' Lem sprang forwards to snatch tickets from the coffee table.

'You better believe it,' said Laura. 'This place is too

heavy for me. I'm going back to the peace and quiet of Hollywood.'

'What shall I tell Nigel,' Lem asked as he gathered her coat and hurried towards the door, 'when he wakes up?'

'Just tell him I feel real sorry for him,' said Laura, 'stuck with someone like Belinda. She's one tough cookie.'

'She ain't really,' said Lem, grinning. 'You just caught her on a really good day, didn't you?'

He decided the BMW was the car for this particular journey and drove Laura to Gatwick at alarming speed. He returned at a more leisurely pace to find Nigel recovering from the shocks and the sedatives with the aid of a Sony Walkman that for reasons best known to himself he was listening to in a semi-foetal position behind the sofa. Lem left him to it and settled down to peruse a comic until a knock at the door disturbed him. He let Belinda in.

'The front door isn't usually locked,' she remarked.

'No,' agreed Lem, 'but I thought it was a good idea until Laura was definitely out of the country.'

'Ah, she hasn't left us, has she?' enquired Belinda insincerely. 'And she didn't even say "so long".'

'You really put the wind up her,' chuckled Lem. 'It was a savage going over. A real turn-up for the book.'

'Yes, wasn't it?' Belinda smiled at the pleasurable memory. 'Of course, I had had a brandy or two.'

'Yeah.' Lem nodded sagely. 'Of course, the £10,000 Nigel bunged her helped.'

'I know I was extremely rude to Nigel,' said Belinda with less authority in her voice now that there was less brandy in her system.

'No more than he deserved,' said Lem.

'I really ought to apologize to him.' Belinda glanced around the room. 'Is he out?'

'Yeah,' grinned Lem. 'Out to lunch.'

'But it's only half past ten,' Belinda frowned.

'Just a figure of speech, doll.' Lem went on grinning as he led Belinda over to the sofa and pointed out the doleful figure smiling wanly from its hiding place.

Belinda smiled. 'Little man, you've had a busy day.'

5

Laura successfully disposed of, life at the Grange settled back into its normal erratic pattern. Nigel continued his piano lessons and his pursuit of Belinda. Belinda continued to teach Nigel, who improved daily, and to prevaricate on the question of to bed or not to bed. Oliver continued to fulminate and Lem, well, Lem just carried on: there was an end in sight. Nigel was talking of going on the road again, which created the need for a name.

'Plutonium,' Lem suggested over the tiddlywinks board.

'Plutonium?' queried Nigel.

'Heavy metal. Radioactivity. Menace.'

'No, Lem. Too seventies,' Nigel said disparagingly. 'We want an eighties image. How does China Syndrome grab you?'

'Yeah, yeah,' said a somewhat piqued Lem. 'Terrific name. For a takeaway.'

'All right then,' said a piqued-in-turn Nigel, 'you come up with something.'

'I still don't know what's wrong with calling us The Nigel Cochrane Band,' said Lem.

''Cos it's so boring,' said the retiring rock star. 'Anyway, I don't want my name bandied around like that. Too high profile.'

'High Profile's not a bad name for a band,' said Lem hopefully.

'Leave it out, Lem,' Nigel said dismissively.

'Leave It Out ain't a bad name for an album,' said an unabashed Lem.

'I wish I hadn't brought the subject up,' Nigel said despairingly.

'I wish I . . .' Lem said, then shrugged. 'Well, if we're going back on the road we've gotta have a name to paint on all that – posters, badges, tee shirts, publicity. All that stuff.'

'Listen to you,' grinned Nigel. 'You're like a kid about to go on his holidays.'

'You can't blame me for being on a high,' announced a happy Lem. 'The road's in my blood. The motels, the freeways, the free women, the adulation, the roar of 50,000 screaming kids . . . Nigel! Nigel!'

His vision of the tour was carrying him away. Far from Churston Deckle and the tranquil, or as Lem would have put it, boring life of the Home Counties. Away to the realm of room service and illegal substances where the beat beat faster and the women were not only willing but didn't wear twinsets and pearls.

Nigel brought him back to earth. 'Lem,' he said wearily, 'before you go over the top, we're not planning a thirty-nine city coast-to-coast tour of the States. We're doing eight polytechnics in the Home Counties. We'll be back here most nights in time for bed.'

'Coming home?' gaped a horrified Lem.

'You really are desperate, aren't you, to return to the debauchery and depravity of the turbulent seventies?' Nigel sounded almost sympathetic.

'I am, Nige,' confirmed an earnest Lem. 'I am. I want that.'

'Okay.' Nigel was magnanimous. 'Just for you – the last night of the tour we'll stay over in a motel in Ruislip.'

'Don't knock Ruislip!' Lem was undeterred. 'Did all right there.'

'Did we?' Nigel couldn't remember.

'Well, I did.' Lem smiled with fond reminiscence.

'Winter Tour, seventy-two. Student nurse. Pauline. Petite and vivacious. Ambitions were to meet Michael Crawford and work with handicapped children.'

'At least she ended up with a legless roadie,' remarked Nigel.

'Happy days, though.' A smile wreathed Lem's features, then faded. 'In sharp contrast to now. Since Belinda came on the scene, it's been like roadying for Cliff Richard.'

'Don't you knock Belinda,' warned Nigel sharply.

'Fat chance,' chortled Lem.

'It's only because of her that I'm even contemplating doing a tour,' Nigel declared. 'She's given me confidence in my own music.'

'It's very nice of you to say so, Nigel,' said Belinda as she walked into the room.

'Oh,' said a mildly surprised Nigel. 'Hello.'

'We're going back on the road,' said an excited Lem.

'Maybe,' Nigel amended.

'You're going to do a concert tour?' Belinda sounded disappointed as she distributed Smarties.

'I'm thinking about it,' nodded Nigel. 'The master's finished except for the final mix and over-dubs, so it's really time to put a gigging band together.'

'Organize rigs, trucks and desks,' expanded Lem. 'Generate some buzz on the streets.'

Belinda gathered that this meant Nigel had composed sufficient new numbers to fill an album and recorded them on tape ready for any additional instrumentation to be added and was now thinking of forming a group to take on tour in the trucks organized by Lem, who would also arrange publicity. 'Have you ever considered compiling a dictionary?' she asked.

'Yeah,' said Lem. 'And Nigel reckons it's all down to you.'

'What is?' asked Belinda, who was feeling confused, not least by the way she felt about Nigel going on tour, which would, presumably, take him away from Churston Deckle.

'You've helped him get his act together on the old keyboard,' Lem explained. 'Shown him where to put his hands. And where not to put them.'

'I'm flattered,' smiled Belinda who wasn't sure she was. 'But I hope this doesn't mean you'll be leaving Churston Deckle for good?'

'No, course not,' Nigel said quickly. 'Anyhow, I want you to come with us.'

'Me?' Belinda was no longer confused. She was bewildered.

'Her?' So was Lem.

'Yeah, right.' Nigel was calm. 'Moral support.'

'Morals on the road?' Lem was horrified at the thought.

'I'm sorry, Nigel,' said a misunderstanding Belinda, 'but I don't see myself in the role of groupie, thank you.'

'Groupie?' Nigel shook his head. 'Don't be daft! You're a great keyboard player – I want you to join my band.'

Belinda gazed at him. He *was* serious which left her in an even greater state of confusion than before. Not long ago she had told her father that Nigel represented a chance to break out of the set mould of life in Churston Deckle, that he accepted her as an individual. Now here was the chance, and not as some hanger-on, but as a bona fide member of the band. But on the other hand there was Oliver, who when she told him, looked up from his wheelchair with Arnold the geranium in one hand and a trowel in the other and his mouth open in between and said, 'I don't know what to say. I'm appalled! The man's a degenerate monster! To ask my daughter to go on the street!'

'Not on the street,' corrected Belinda. 'On the road.'

'Street, road,' said Oliver dismissively, 'it's all prostitution.'

'For God's sake, Daddy!' Belinda felt angry: this was, after all, her big chance.

'Language,' admonished Oliver sternly.

'Going on the road,' Belinda explained with remarkable restraint, 'means playing in Nigel's group.'

'What? You mean busking?' Oliver gasped in dumbfounded, or nearly, horror. 'One step away from vagrancy.'

'I haven't even agreed to go.' Belinda felt her resolve falter as usual before her father's onslaught. 'But I think it was jolly nice of Nigel to ask, and I told him I would think it over.'

'In that case, all is not lost,' said Oliver in relieved tones. 'You must reject him forthwith.'

'Why should I?' queried a defensive Belinda. 'It might be fun playing before a paying audience. I used to enjoy giving recitals.'

'Belle,' said Oliver with the passive authority of disinformation, 'he is not asking you to play Chopin etudes to the Women's Institute. You'll be expected to cavort before thousands of drug-crazed Communists.'

'At Guildford Polytechnic Students' Union?' asked Belinda, reasonably enough.

'Precisely,' nodded Oliver sagaciously. 'You only have his word that Guildford will be your destination. Before the war Binky Heyhoe's sister Candida had ambitions in the ballet. An oily agent chappy promised her a part in *Les Sylphides* at Sadler's Wells. Binky waved the girl off from Dorking Station and he never saw her again until years later, when he was with the Eighth Army in Libya, and found her employed in a house of ill repute in Tripoli.'

He sat back, pleased with the enlightening nature of his anecdote. It was an enlightenment Belinda found less than illuminating. 'A fascinating story,' she admitted, 'but I'm a grown woman and I'm not going to allow you to tyrannize me any longer. I will make up my mind about Nigel's offer in my own good time, and I will not be influenced by horror stories of the white slave trade in Dorking.'

Oliver saw the very foundations of his comfortable life assaulted, undermined by the foul blandishments of the yobbo singer. Whisk his innocent Belinda away on some degenerate mystery tour where unspeakable things might threaten to besmirch her? Not while he was there to protect her. It was his duty. And besides, how on earth would he cope on his own? 'Very well,' he said firmly, demonstrating the reluctant authority of a parent looking after his child's best interests, 'I can see you are infatuated beyond reason. I shall go personally to the Grange and confront Cochrane man to beast. Help me start my car.'

'Don't be silly, Daddy,' warned Belinda.

'That's an order!' Danger caused Oliver to regress to his Headmasterly approach as he stumped out of the conservatory.

Sighing, Belinda followed him to where his lovingly-tended Rover sat glistening, only the polished paintwork belying its twenty-five years. Oliver was already stooped over the starting handle.

'You're wasting your time,' Belinda commented. 'This wreck hasn't started for months.'

'Wreck?' Oliver was an Englishman. His home was his castle and a slight to his car was an insult to his person. 'Nonsense! She's a fine old English motor car, built in the heyday of British engineering. Which of today's Nipponese egg-boxes-on-wheels can boast such gleaming chrome, lustrous paintwork, leather upholstery, walnut dash?'

'Pity the engine's buggered.' Circumstance enlarged Belinda's vocabulary.

'Good God!' gasped Oliver in stricken tones. 'I never thought I'd hear barrack room language from my daughter's lips. Obviously picked it up from Cochrane and his sybarites at the Grange. And she wonders why I forbid her to join the wretched man's jazz band.' Sadly he gazed at her. 'I never thought you, Belinda, would sink so low so quickly.'

Belinda found that she was, unusually, unwilling to bandy words with her father; even less usually, she was not prepared to concede. 'Why don't you face facts?' she asked. 'There's about as much life left in this car as there is in the . . .' She searched for the most suitable simile and found it in, 'the British Empire.'

Change and decay were augmented by rebellion. 'How dare you denigrate our country's greatness?' barked a wrathful Oliver. 'Look at any atlas: half the world is still coloured red.'

'Yes,' Belinda allowed, 'but that's the Communist half.'

'We've still got Gibraltar, Hong Kong, Ascension and the Falklands.' Oliver found he was suddenly on the defensive. Put like that, the list didn't sound very long.

'Not to mention Tristan da Cunha and the Isle of Man,' Belinda compounded her insult.

'Get in the damn' cockpit and get ready to rev up when I crank,' snapped Oliver.

'Crank being the operative word,' muttered Belinda as she climbed into the aforementioned cockpit and prepared to rev up.

'Gears disengaged?' asked Oliver.

'Since before Christmas,' replied Belinda.

Oliver grunted and stooped to the starting handle. Nothing happened when he turned it, so he turned it again and grunted again. Then cried out as a pain shot through a hip, and clutched at the polished bonnet. Belinda climbed out and came to watch him as he hunched over.

'Sudden stabbing pain.'

'Yes, I'm sure, Daddy.' It didn't sound as though she believed him: she didn't. 'When it comes to playing the old soldier, you are Chief of the General Staff.'

And with that she walked off.

The plan went ahead. For the first time in her life Belinda was ready, not to mention willing and able, to defy Oliver. She had told Nigel she would play keyboards on the tour and he had found musicians to build around that focus. Lem had organized the gigs and it was time for full scale practice in the Grange. Everyone except Belinda was ready. A drummer sat idly knocking out paradiddles while two guitarists drank beer and Lem checked the mixing desk. Nigel stood by an interior door trying to persuade Belinda to come out.

'Come on,' he urged. 'Honest, Belinda, you look terrific. Just like Liza Minnelli.'

'What?' asked a disbelieving Lem. 'You got her into stockings and suspenders?'

'Shut it, Lem!' snapped Nigel. Then to the door, 'Come on, love.'

The door opened and a nervous Belinda emerged wearing evening dress: stiff shirt, bow tie and tails. The band applauded. Belinda was less certain of the effect. 'You solemnly swear we'll all be wearing tails?' she asked.

'Cross my heart,' swore Nigel, eyeing her approvingly. 'It does need altering here and there. After all, you're not the sort of shape Moss Bros usually deals with. Give us a twirl.' Belinda twirled. 'Smart, eh?'

'Oh, very,' smiled Belinda, catching his enthusiasm. 'If a trifle androgenous.'

'You what?' frowned Lem.

'Bisexual,' supplied Nigel.

'No?!' Lem assumed an expression of shock. 'And she looks so feminine.'

The drummer tapped out a roll and Nigel rounded on him, 'You shut it an' all, Reg, or you'll be out on your tom-toms.' There was silence and Nigel looked round pleadingly. 'I thought a bit of class would make a nice change. Besides, I always thought it was hypocritical when we used to dress like bums and get fifty grand a night.'

The bassist gaped, visions of wealth flashing before his widening eyes. 'Fifty grand?' he said in a wondering voice.

'Calm down, Denny,' soothed Nigel. 'That was the Hollywood Bowl, not the Guildford saucer.'

'I suppose even Daddy couldn't object to this attire,' remarked Belinda, thus causing hoots of merriment from the group who were, as yet, more accustomed to the world of pop music than that of Churston Deckle.

'All right,' Nigel warned them again. 'How is he, by the way?'

'As an actor he's never been better,' said Belinda caustically. 'Ever since the starting handle incident, he's been a piteous sight to behold.'

'You've got to admit Daddy is a tryer,' said Lem.

'You sure he is putting it on?' asked Nigel.

'I should know him,' replied Belinda. 'He's my father.'

'Fair enough.' Nigel turned to face the group. 'Right. Shall we have a go at the opening ditty?'

The guitarists plugged in their instruments and took a tune check. Lem settled behind the mixing desk. Nigel took up position at the synthesizer and Belinda stood behind an upright piano. Derek, the lead guitarist, asked, 'Can you give us an E, darling?' And Belinda blew his doubts away with an elaborate arpeggio. 'One would have done.'

They began to play, Nigel singing the narrative as the others came in on chorus:

'She will,' sang Nigel, answered by all with, 'Tell you lies.'

'But she's organized with the boys.
She told me she loved me,
She won't let me go.
She kissed me in public,
But everyone knows she's been
Working out with the boys again.
Working out with the boys.
She will
Tell you lies,
But she's organized with the boys.
Now understand, I'm fooling myself.
I'm just half a man,
I'm hanging on.
She's wrong for me.
She's too strong for me and she's
Stringing me along.
But she crucifies,
Nails me with her lies.
And she's organized with the boys.'

They were all going into another chorus when the telephone rang and Lem moved to answer. He listened through the music, then shouted for quiet. 'Anyone got a connection goes by the name of Doc Rutherford?'

'Oh, God!' Belinda went promptly pale. 'It's for me!'

'Great!' said Reg. 'Can you get us some uppers?'

'Sorry?' Belinda frowned as she took the phone.

Doctor Rutherford had heard – with a surgery in Churston Deckle how could he not? – that Oliver Purcell's Belinda was consorting with the rock musician who had taken over the Grange. That the man's influence should cause her to wear masculine evening dress in the afternoon was, he assumed as she hurried into her father's bedroom, one of those things that happened in the music world. 'I just thought I would look in on your father,' he explained somewhat disapprovingly. 'Purely a social call. It was fortunate Mrs Hammersley has a spare key to your front door.'

'And I thought it was all a sham.' Belinda stared in horrified guilt at Oliver who for once, thanks to Doctor Rutherford's sedation, did not contest the point. 'Oh, I feel so awful!'

'Don't blame yourself, my dear,' soothed the doctor. 'After all, your father is county champion lead swinger. And with a plastic hip joint he'll be as good as new. I've given him something to help him sleep, so he's a little woozy.'

On cue, Oliver asked drowsily, 'Belle, is that you?'

'Oh, Daddy.' Belinda crossed to the bedside, guilt writ large on her pretty face. 'I'm so sorry.'

'I'm going, Belinda,' quavered Oliver. 'I can hear the angels.'

'No,' said Belinda, 'it's the wireless.'

'I'm coming, Amelia,' Oliver told the ceiling.

'Stuff and nonsense, Purcell,' said Doctor Rutherford briskly. 'Nothing wrong with you that a polythene pelvis won't put right.'

'I'm not dying?' demanded a mildly disappointed Oliver.

'Of course not,' assured Rutherford.

'Then why,' asked Oliver as he stared at Belinda's evening suited figure, 'is the undertaker here?'

Nigel was attempting uselessly to telephone Belinda when she walked into the living room of the Grange no longer clad in tie and tails and devoid also of her earlier excitement. She was, by contrast, distinctly subdued.

'Oh, I was just about to call you,' said Nigel. 'Is he all right?'

'Well,' said Belinda cautiously, 'yes and no.'

'He's not dead then?' enquired Lem cheerfully.

'Knock it off, Lem.' Nigel saw that Belinda was genuinely worried.

'It's a hip joint,' she told him.

'We like it.' Lem glanced around the room. 'Mind you, it's nowhere near as hip as Rod's place in Malibu. That's really hip.'

'Lem was just going to make some tea,' Nigel said pointedly. 'Prior to looking for a new job.'

Lem could take a hint. 'You were saying?' Nigel said as he left the room.

'Apparently the hip has just worn out and seized up,' Belinda explained.

'Sounds like a car,' remarked Nigel.

'We have one of those, too,' Belinda replied wistfully. 'It doesn't go either.'

'So what are you gonna do about it?' Nigel was thinking about the tour.

'Sorry?' Belinda smiled absent-mindedly. 'Oh, I suppose we'll have it towed away sometime.'

'What?' asked Nigel. 'Your Dad?'

'No, no, the car,' said Belinda. 'Daddy needs an op, apparently. But he'll have to wait his turn.'

'How long for?' Nigel could envisage Oliver thwarting his plans yet.

'I don't know.' Belinda shook her head. 'The N.H.S. seem loath to commit themselves to an actual date.'

'But we're going on the road next week!'

There was desperation in Nigel's voice. It was not helped by Belinda's reply.

'*You're* going on the road. My rock and roll debut will have to be postponed.'

'Then I'll call the tour off,' announced Nigel.

'That's absurd,' Belinda pointed out. 'I'm sure there are hundreds of pianists who would jump at the chance to take my place.'

'But I don't want any old pianist,' countered Nigel plaintively. 'I want you! Look, why doesn't your Dad have the op privately?'

'Because,' said Belinda, 'strange as it may seem, we can't afford it.'

The inability to afford something so simple as a Harley Street operation was a disadvantage with which Nigel had grown unfamiliar. He was surprised. 'Straight up?' he asked with a look of astonishment.

'Straight up,' agreed Belinda. 'Unless I sell my pearls.'

'No need for that. I'll lend you the money.' Nigel turned to shout, 'Lem! Wallet! How much would it cost?'

'I don't know,' murmured Belinda. 'At least three or four thousand. We could never pay you back.'

'Then don't pay me back,' said Nigel carelessly.

'We can't accept charity,' Belinda told him.

'Don't think of it as charity,' grinned Nigel. 'Think of it as friendship. Anyway, I earned more than that in Japanese royalties last night while I was asleep.'

'You're very sweet.' Belinda smiled at him, appreciating

his generosity. 'But you know how firmly my father clings to his principles.'

'Like despising me, for example,' muttered Nigel.

'He doesn't despise you,' Belinda said defensively. 'He just despises what you stand for.'

'Oh, that's charming!' Nigel was hurt.

'Those are his words,' Belinda reassured him, 'not mine.'

'I'm not so sure.' Nigel was dubious. Not yet convinced that this was not another devious subterfuge of Oliver's with which Belinda was complying.

'What do you mean?' she demanded, feeling hurt in turn.

'If that's not how you feel, too,' he said sulkily.

'Then it seems you don't know me very well!' snapped Belinda.

'You tell me, love,' Nigel suggested.

'I've already told you!' She was angry now, guessing what he was thinking and resenting it all the more for the element of truth it held. 'I do have a mind of my own, you know.'

'Then take the bloody money and put him out of his misery,' urged Nigel not unreasonably.

'Don't yell at me,' yelled Belinda. 'You're worse than Daddy.'

Nigel stared at her and she stared at him and after a while they both began to wonder what they were quarrelling about.

'Sorry,' said Nigel gently. 'I was only trying to help out.'

'I know,' said Belinda apologetically. 'It's just . . . Well, he won't accept hand-outs.'

Nigel's amiable face became cunning. 'Then we'll have to be a bit slippery, won't we?' he grinned. 'A bit devious.'

* * *

Having accepted the less-than-imminent nature of his demise, Oliver had applied his energies to the problem of securing a hospital bed, deciding as usual that the best way was a letter to *The Times*. He was just finishing as Belinda came into the bedroom with a vase of spring flowers.

'Ah, Belle!' he declared happily. 'Just the chap. Listen to this.' He cleared his throat importantly. 'The Editor, *The Times*, Printing House Square, etcetera, etcetera. Sir, when we elected a Conservative government we were assured they would bring order and efficiency into the running of the National Health Service. Why then must I, a life-long Tory voter, who served his country in two world wars, be made to wait several months for a simple operation?'

'Daddy, you were only eleven when the First World War ended,' Belinda pointed out.

'Nonetheless, I volunteered to fight,' said Oliver indignantly. 'But they turned me down.'

'I imagine your short trousers gave the game away,' Belinda suggested.

'No, I was tall for my age.' Oliver paused ruminatively. 'If only Nanny hadn't insisted on coming to the War Office with me. Now, to continue.'

'Not now, Daddy,' Belinda interrupted before he was able to gather steam again. 'You've a visitor.'

'It's not the Reverend Sclater-Booth again, is it?' asked Oliver in some alarm.

'No,' said Belinda rather warily, which was understandable in the circumstances of Oliver's injury, 'it's Nigel. Mr Cochrane.'

'Tell him I'm not in,' barked the invalid a fraction too late as Nigel's cheery face was already appearing around the door.

'Hello, governor,' he said, perhaps a trifle nervously. 'Just thought I'd pop round and see how you were doing.'

'I'm doing as well as can be expected,' said Oliver as his visitor entered the room. 'Good day.'

'Don't be so rude, Daddy,' Belinda reprimanded. 'Come in, Nigel.'

Nigel came all the way in, in a manner not dissimilar to that of a man invited to enter a confined space in company with a dangerous animal. He held a wrapped bottle in his hand and a cautious smile on his lips.

'I brought you a bottle of brandy,' he said. 'Belinda said you like the occasional belt. For medicinal purposes only,' he added quickly.

Oliver took the bottle and was impressed by the label enough to murmur reluctantly, 'Thank you. It's very civil of you.'

'Sorry about the hip and all that,' sympathized Nigel. 'Does it hurt much?'

'Of course not,' answered Oliver acidly. 'I intend to go ballroom dancing this evening.'

'Point taken,' Nigel apologized. 'I'll be off then.' He paused, a fraction dramatically. 'Oh, by the way. I don't suppose you know who owns that old Rover out front, do you?'

'Why?' Oliver was instantly alert. 'If you've run into her . . .'

'No, it's just I was admiring it.' Nigel glanced casually through the bedroom window to where the car sat. 'Very tasty motor. Rover 80 with a flat four side valve power unit and lateral pushrods. Very rare specimen.'

'Really?' This casual display of automotive expertise impressed Oliver, particularly as it was his car on the receiving end of Nigel's detailed attention. 'You're a connoisseur of fine cars?'

'Yeah,' Nigel grinned, crossing his fingers, 'me and Lord Montague are like that.'

'The Rover's ours,' offered Belinda somewhat stagily.

'No?' Nigel pantomimed surprise. 'Really?' And turning to Oliver, he asked, 'You know it's a real collector's item?'

'Er . . . um . . . of course,' bluffed Oliver, 'I know.'

'I don't suppose you'd consider selling it?'

'Well, I don't know,' demurred Oliver as a cunning gleam lit his eyes. 'There's a great deal of sentiment involved. My late lamented wife and I used to go everywhere in the dear old thing, and when I sit in the driver's seat – real hide, you know – it's almost as if Amelia is still there beside me.'

'I'll give you four thousand for it,' said Nigel.

'Belinda,' said Oliver, 'the log book's in the tallboy.'

The scheme worked. At least, with the four thousand pounds handed over Oliver disappeared into hospital with no further delays, which left Belinda free to continue practising with the band and Nigel without fear that her father would, like some pantomime villain, pop up to thwart his plans. It also left Belinda free to spend more time with Nigel, an opportunity she enjoyed taking full advantage of. Amongst other things, it gave her a chance to sprawl on the floor of her own home eating fish and chips in a manner sufficiently abandoned that Oliver would never have permitted it.

'Absolutely sublime,' she sighed as she rolled greasy paper into a ball. 'I wouldn't be allowed to eat bought fish and chips if Daddy were here.'

'There are lots of things you wouldn't be able to do if Daddy were here,' Nigel commented. 'How's he finding the plastic hip?'

'It's fantastic,' said Belinda. 'Though he is a little miffed it's plastic. I think he'd prefer it if it were leather with walnut veneer.'

'Well,' shrugged Nigel, 'that's what you get with Japanese plastic hips flooding the country.'

'You know I'm really grateful, Nigel?' Her voice was earnest.

'Any chance of your demonstrating your gratitude?' he asked softly.

'How?' Belinda asked, knowing the answer.

'A cuddle would be okay for starters,' Nigel said, moving closer when he saw she didn't object. He kissed her and felt her respond, then pull away. 'What's wrong?'

'Nothing is wrong, Nigel.' Belinda shook her head. 'It's just that this is Daddy's home.'

'But Daddy's not home,' Nigel argued. 'And it's your home, too.'

'That makes it worse.' Belinda was caught in a dilemma of Oliver's making. 'I feel I'm betraying his trust.'

'Bloody hell! I don't believe it!' Nigel snorted, cursing the spectre of Oliver that loomed suddenly large in the cosy drawing room. 'That man's more aggravation when he's not here! This is the twentieth century and you are not a nun! Why don't we go back to my place then?'

'Is that the only thing you're interested in?' asked Belinda dubiously. 'Kissing?'

'Not the only thing,' Nigel answered honestly, 'no.'

'Because I was foolish enough to believe that you actually liked me for myself.'

'You know I do!' Nigel's voice rose in protest as he felt the moment melt away under Oliver's shadow. 'But I don't want you to be my sister.'

'While we're in this village,' said Belinda with reluctant firmness, 'that's all that's on offer.'

'Supposing we went somewhere else?' asked Nigel hopefully.

'I've heard about the things groups get up to on the road,' Belinda said mischievously.

'I've heard them an' all,' nodded Nigel. 'I wonder if they're true.'

Preparations for the tour went ahead. With no other choice, Nigel accepted that any development in his relationship with Belinda was going to happen outside the confines of Churston Deckle, which made him all the more eager to be on his way. A week after his frustrating evening with Belinda, he listened to Lem briefing the road crew.

'So that's transport, catering, publicity, security, alcohol, accommodation.' Lem checked the items on a clipboard as the crew ambled out. 'Hang on! Just as well I'm a demon for detail – I've just spotted a cock-up. We're a bedroom short at Newcastle. They don't seem to have a reservation for Belinda.'

'Oh yeah?' Nigel said innocently. 'I suppose someone will have to double up.'

'You dirty old superstar,' remarked Lem.

'What?' Nigel seemed blind to ulterior motives. Was it, Lem wondered, Belinda's influence?

At which point she walked in. Nigel said, 'That's what I like: eagerness. You're a day early, but never mind.'

'I can't come!' said Belinda desperately.

'Very funny,' said Nigel.

'I'm sorry, but I mean it. I'm afraid Daddy . . .'

Nigel found this hard to take. 'Now what's wrong with him?' he asked nervously.

'Nothing,' said Belinda. 'He couldn't be better. But the surgeon told him to go away to convalesce and he needs me to roadie for him. I am sorry, but he does come first.'

With which she abruptly exited, as though afraid Nigel might explode or perhaps dissuade her. Nigel was too confused to do either. All he could muster was a cry of, 'Hey, Belinda!'

'I knew this would happen,' Lem remarked philosophically. 'Linda McCartney's got a lot to answer for. Nige, don't panic!'

But Nigel was already rushing after Belinda like a man chasing an extremely elusive butterfly which was fluttering fast down the steps to the brand new second hand car from whose paintwork a proud Oliver was carefully flicking specks of invisible dust.

'Look,' Nigel cried, 'what's going on?'

'Good day to you, Mr Cochrane,' Oliver said with the generosity of the victor.

'Nigel, there's nothing more to add,' said Belinda guiltily. 'I'm sorry, but . . .'

'Yes, I'm glad to say I've made an excellent recovery from my operation,' Oliver continued briskly. 'It was good of you to enquire.'

Nigel gaped at him, unable to believe that at this late moment Oliver had still succeeded. It was like the Seventh Cavalry riding in to the rescue. With Nigel cast as the Indians. 'All right, you devious old . . .' he began. 'How have you nobbled her this time?'

'Nobbled?' Oliver frowned politely. Too politely. 'I've simply asked my daughter to accompany me on a fortnight's recuperative vacation at the Grand Hotel, Eastbourne.'

'I have to go,' said Belinda plaintively. 'He's my father.'

'And what about my tour?' Nigel gestured at the big van with *Nigel Cochrane and Plutonium* emblazoned down the side.

'You don't need me,' said Belinda, hoping he'd agree

and knowing he wouldn't, but not knowing what else to say. 'You're really good enough to play all the keyboard parts yourself.'

'But I'm not ready.' It was Nigel's turn to sound plaintive. 'I've never played anything in public but the bass guitar.' He turned angrily to Oliver. 'And I thought you was skint! How can you afford flash hotels? And how did you lay your hands on this motor?'

'You paid for it, Mr Cochrane,' said Oliver with infinite satisfaction.

'Believe me, Nigel,' said Belinda hurriedly as Nigel's jaw descended towards his chest. 'I honestly didn't know.'

'Know what?' asked a shattered superstar.

'It was probably my letter to *The Times* that stirred things up,' smiled Oliver with the air of a man who has successfully completed a difficult exercise. 'Suddenly the National Health desk jockeys found me a free bed. Stroke of luck, what? So the money you gave me for the Rover was all cash in hand.'

He nodded smugly as he settled into the car, leaving Nigel standing with his mouth open. 'Come on, Belle. Let us take a drive into Dorking. You can help me choose a couple of lightweight suits from Dunn and Co.'

Belinda stared helplessly at Nigel, shrugged, and started the car. Oliver sat back happily. All was well in his world. Order was restored.

'I suppose you want me to cancel the whole nobbing tour now?' asked Lem as the car disappeared down the drive and Nigel wrung his hands together with an expression of pure panic on his knobby features. But to the roadie's surprise Nigel shook his head.

'You must be joking! I'm not giving in as easy as that. Lem, get us a gig in Eastbourne!'

Lem goggled. 'They're all O. A. P.s and hearing aids in Eastbourne.'

'I pay the wages,' said Nigel petulantly. 'Get us a gig in Eastbourne.'

'Anyway,' said Lem, trying hard to avoid Eastbourne, 'they've put a block on shows in Eastbourne. Last time a star was there the fans ripped all the seats up.'

'Oh, yeah?' asked a dubious Nigel. 'Who was that then?'

'Donald Piers!' said Lem and saw the joke wasn't working. 'No, but I mean what are you going to do? "Begin The Beguine"?'

'Shut up, Lem,' ordered a determined Nigel.

6

'Hello, old chap. The neighbour's not been overwatering you, I trust?' Oliver enquired of Arnold as he limped briskly into the conservatory. 'Eastbourne was quite pleasant, thank you. Weather a trifle changeable. Much rain here? Oh no, of course, you wouldn't know, you're a house plant.'

'I've taken the cases upstairs, Daddy,' said Belinda, entering the conservatory with a rather less sprightly air.

'Splendid,' said Oliver, adding magnanimously, 'You needn't unpack them until after you've made some tea.'

'Too kind,' Belinda muttered, moving towards the door with one hand behind her back.

'What have you got there?' Oliver demanded.

'Nothing,' said Belinda.

'What are you hiding behind your back?'

'Oh, just a few postcards.'

'Then why are you hiding them?'

His reasonableness was infuriating. Belinda blushed. 'Because they're from Nigel and they're private.'

'Poppycock!' declared Oliver. 'Postcards are de facto in the public realm. Everyone knows the postman reads them all. If Cochrane wanted to be confidential he should have sent you a letter.'

'And put you to the trouble of steaming open the envelope?' Belinda asked with sarcastic innocence.

'I wouldn't dream of doing anything so underhand,' protested an affronted Oliver. 'If I wish to read your letters I open them with my paper knife.'

'You're nothing if not blatant,' said Belinda.

'There should be no secrets within a family,' announced Oliver, snatching the cards from her and holding them high in the air as she strove uselessly to snatch them back. 'Good heavens! Joined up writing! "Essex University. Another bum gig, audience a pig." Well, that solves the problem of who should succeed Sir John Betjeman as Poet Laureate.'

'Sometimes, Daddy!' cried Belinda angrily as Oliver chuckled at his own wit, and stormed furiously out.

'You know, Vincent, the younger generation has no sense of humour,' Oliver informed a rubber plant and settled happily into his wheelchair to read Belinda's postcards. 'Croydon, Leicester, Hollywood? Oh,' he paused to check the postcard, 'the Birmingham Hollywood. Warwickshire.'

As he read the chronicle of the concert tour, its star and its organizer were settled back into the Grange. Nigel was staring out of the window brooding on the tour, which he did not consider had been the success he wanted. Chiefly because Belinda hadn't been on it with him. Lem was busily telephoning, the call raising his spirits to the point where he was chortling with anticipation as he set the phone down.

'Henry's having a bit of a birthday thrash down Longfellows, Wednesday night.'

'You know I hate nightclubs, Lem,' said Nigel in a querulous voice.

'I wouldn't mind you being a bit manic depressive,' remarked Lem, 'if only you'd be a bit manic once in a while.'

'The tour was a total disaster,' said Nigel gloomily.

'The tour was a total disaster,' parroted Lem. 'Look, we packed the colleges, we did a lot of encores, we showed a profit.'

'As far as I'm concerned the whole sound was terrible,' moaned Nigel. 'It was too thin. What we really missed was Belinda on keyboards.'

'Blimey!' said Lem in some surprise as realization dawned for the first time. 'I never realized you was so stuck on her.'

'Neither did I,' admitted Nigel dolefully.

'She's turned you into a right royal pain in the bum, hasn't she?' offered the roadie. 'If you want my opinion . . .'

'Thanks very much, Lem,' Nigel said quickly. 'But when I seek advice to the lovelorn, I'll consult Marje Proops, not an undersized, oversexed roadie.'

Lem was hurt by this dismissal. 'And who was it who saved you from a nasty misunderstanding with that fifteen stone woofter in Burrow-in-Furness?' he demanded. 'This undersized, oversexed roadie here.'

'That's what you're paid for,' said Nigel callously.

Enough was enough. Lem had found this hermitage for Nigel, he had sheltered the rock star from the depredations of the press, he had pulled all the stops organizing the tour, and the tour had – amazingly in this day and age and hard times – shown a profit. He had shared Nigel's monastic existence – well, almost – and he had nursed Nigel through his paranoia over piano lessons, through Laura's visit; he'd even tried to book a gig in Eastbourne, beyond which he could envisage no greater sacrifice. And now, when Nigel should be feeling pleased, the miserable Orson was as miserable as ever and insulting his loyal roadie to boot. 'You bloody, steaming wobbist,' Lem cried, and jumped on his boss.

They proceeded to grapple around the room, engaging in this activity as Belinda entered, hot from her altercation with Oliver.

'What on earth are you two doing?' she asked alarmedly.

'We're making war, not love,' replied Lem, holding Nigel firmly in a headlock as Nigel bellowed, 'Let go, you bastard!'

'Nigel!' Belinda admonished. 'Language!'

'Sod language!' said an unrepentant rock star. 'I'm choking here. Lem, you're sacked!'

The news failed to deter the angry roadie. Nigel's nose began to bleed. Belinda ordered, 'Let him go, Lem.'

Lem said, 'Not till he says sorry.'

'Nigel, say sorry,' said Belinda.

Nigel said, 'He started it.'

And they began struggling again until Belinda seized an ear in either hand and hauled them bodily, or at least earily, apart.

'Now sit there,' she commanded, depositing them on separate chairs, 'and tell me why you were fighting.'

'We weren't fighting. Lem attacked me,' Nigel protested, then realized his nose was bleeding and cried mournfully, 'You've given me one of my nosebleeds now.'

Belinda passed him a handkerchief which he pressed to his nose as he tilted his head back to stare at the ceiling. 'Tie a rope round your neck,' suggested Lem unsympathetically, 'that'll stop it. You've hurt my ear.' And clutching the wounded portion of his anatomy he left the room.

Nigel peered at the bloodstained handkerchief as though afraid his life was draining away and said, 'I think I need to lend another hankie.'

'Borrow,' Belinda corrected, passing him paper tissues. 'Oh, I've brought you a present from Eastbourne.'

She passed him a stick of seaside rock that he studied with some difficulty, holding it above his head to squint past the tissue enveloping his nostrils. 'Oh look,' he said, 'it's got "Vote Conservative" all the way through. So what sort of time did you and Daddy have?'

'Oh, he was in his element,' Belinda replied, her gaiety a little nervous. 'Eastbourne's full of people like him.'

'What about you?'

'It was quite nice to be waited on for a fortnight,' she said, knowing that wasn't really what he was asking.

'You didn't meet anyone?' he asked more directly.

'Don't worry,' Belinda assured, smiling, 'no dashing knight in shining armour tried to carry me off in his bath chair.'

This news was good enough for Nigel to remove the tissue long enough to risk looking entreatingly at Belinda.

'So you did miss me?'

'That depends.' Cautiously: Nigel tilted his head back to address the ceiling again.

'I missed you.'

'Did you really?' asked Belinda delightedly.

'We couldn't get anyone else to play keyboards at short notice,' said Nigel.

Belinda said, 'Oh,' in a small voice.

'It would have been nice having you around after the gigs, too,' he added, holding out a hand that Belinda took. 'Hello.'

Belinda began to smile again. Nigel sounded thoughtful: 'You know what would be really nice? If we got together without Lem or Daddy sticking their oars in.'

'That would be a novelty,' said Belinda in a tone that said she didn't entertain much hope of it happening.

'Fancy coming out for dinner tomorrow night?' asked Nigel casually. 'Up in town?'

Belinda's face lit up. 'Dorking?' she asked in tones of wonder.

'Do us a favour.' Nigel felt this was taking the theory that small is beautiful a little far. 'London.'

'Love to,' said Belinda without a second's hesitation.

'Great!' Nigel looked happy for the first time since the last time he saw her.

'Oh,' she remembered now that the major dramas were over, 'I brought you something else from Eastbourne.'

'What, a kiss me quick sun hat?' he asked the ceiling.

'No. They had a piano at the hotel, so I composed a pop song.'

'You're having me on.' Nigel did his best to look sideways without moving his head and found it hard to do, so Belinda extracted a sheet of paper from her handbag and held it above his head. 'Yeah. Well, play it for me then. I won't join you, cos I haven't finished bleeding.'

Leaving him to drip, Belinda crossed to the piano and began to play 'Don't Turn Your Back On The One You Love', which might have been a title inspired by her feelings whilst in Eastbourne. Whether that was so or not, the music was good enough that Nigel decided to risk movement and come over to the piano and Lem re-appeared.

'No words yet,' Belinda apologized as she finished. 'What do you think?'

'Yeah,' nodded an impressed Nigel, 'that's really good.'

'Oh no,' smiled a modest but nonetheless delighted Belinda. 'I wouldn't say that.'

'Neither would I,' sniffed Lem.

'I could use that on this album,' announced Nigel, ignoring them both.

'There you go, Belinda.' Lem sounded sardonic. 'That's how Carole King started. You could be on to untold wealth.'

'Why not?' demanded Nigel aggressively.

'I mean,' continued Lem in the same unpleasant tone, 'a cut on Nigel Cochrane's debut solo album? In this country alone it could sell in dozens.'

It was Nigel's turn to feel insulted. He kicked Lem. The fight started again.

Oliver had no idea that he had an ally in his opposition to Belinda's affair with Nigel and so shouldered alone the task of dissuading his daughter from succumbing to the blandishments of the upstart rock star. But Belinda had discovered somewhere a streak of obstinacy that made Oliver's life difficult.

'You've never been this wilful before, Belle,' he complained. 'Did Cochrane give you anything to smoke? You know Harry and Petulia Vacher are expecting to play bridge tomorrow night.'

'As you never consult me,' remarked Belinda tartly, 'I didn't know.'

'This isn't good enough, Belle,' Oliver declared sternly. 'Suppose he takes you to a nightclub?'

'Oh, do you think he might?' Belinda asked eagerly.

'You wouldn't enjoy it, you know.' Oliver shook his head with the sagacity of one who does know.

'I'll take my chances,' said Belinda bravely.

'Oh, the bravado of the young,' sighed Oliver. 'I remember just before the war a chap Binky Heyhoe's sister Candida once danced with – he came from a good family, but he got caught up in the twilight world of the nightclub, got mixed up with a fast crowd, lost interest in the family business and ran off with an American divorcee.'

'I think you're referring to King Edward VIII, Daddy,' Belinda remarked mildly.

'Exactly!' Oliver pounced on this vital point. 'And if he succumbed to the tawdry blandishments of the Chelsea Set, what hope is there for you?'

* * *

Belinda remained undeterred and the next night was intrigued as Nigel drove to a dark block of buildings somewhere along the western reaches of the river Thames. The place appeared to be a block of flats, but Belinda, whose experience of fashionable London eating places was somewhat limited, was far too excited by the prospect of spending an evening alone with Nigel to question this subdued appearance. At least, until Nigel led the way in to what was obviously an empty apartment.

'Very exclusive here, isn't it?' Belinda looked at the deserted sitting room. 'There can't be many restaurants where customers need a key to the front door. Nigel?' she asked, waiting for an explanation.

'Quite nice though, innit?' offered Nigel, who was himself examining the apartment with the air of a prospective buyer.

'Where exactly are we?' asked a confused Belinda.

'Chelsea,' said Nigel.

'Perhaps Daddy was right,' she murmured. 'Should I consider myself abducted?'

It was a rather exciting thought and she was mildly disappointed when Nigel shook his head and told her, 'No. This is my *pied à terre*,' in an atrocious accent. 'My London bachelor pad.'

'You own this flat?' Belinda was amazed.

'Lock, stock and biscuit barrel,' confirmed her host.

'Then why did you have to ask that policeman directions?'

It seemed a reasonable enough question.

''Cos I've never been here before.' Nigel began to open doors in an interested way. 'You see, we bought the show flat as it stood. I had to get rid of a bit of money end of last tax year. You know how it is.'

'Not really,' Belinda murmured.

'Not bad though, is it?' Nigel continued his exploration. 'Wonder where the kitchen is? I'd fix you a drink if I could find the kitchen.'

Belinda set a row of imitation books back on the shelf and asked somewhat primly, 'Why have you brought me here, Nigel?'

'Dinner,' said Nigel.

'Oh, of course,' said Belinda disbelievingly.

'I mean,' said Nigel cheerfully, 'we agreed we wanted to spend a bit of time together, so I thought it was a good time to check the flat out.' He sounded quite innocent as he crossed to a window. 'Nice view, innit? You see them council flats over the other side of Battersea power station? I used to live there. I done all right, ain't I?'

The simple pride in his voice managed to banish Belinda's fears. She smiled, opening a door. 'Kitchen. I hope you don't expect me to cook for you? Assuming there's anything . . .' She was opening cupboards as she spoke, uncovering a hoard of tins. 'Oh, yes. There's plenty of tinned stuff. Do you have a favourite flavour of cat food?'

'Rabbit for preference,' grinned Nigel, putting an arm around her.

Before Belinda could decide what to do there was a knock at the door. She was not sure whether she was pleased or disappointed by the interruption.

'Probably the cat.' Unperturbed, Nigel opened the door to reveal a white-jacketed waiter wheeling a laden trolley. 'Dinner is served.'

'I'm sure I've seen this in a film,' murmured a not-quite-dumbstruck Belinda as the waiter wheeled his burden past her.

'That's where I got the idea,' admitted Nigel, feeling pleased with himself. 'The kitchen's through there, chief.'

Belinda watched the trolley and the waiter disappear into the kitchen and turned smiling to Nigel. 'Haven't you forgotten something?' she asked teasingly.

'I don't think so.' Nigel shook his head. 'We've got Pacific prawns, wild duck, passion fruit sorbet, a nice Chablis . . . That's about everything.'

'What about the gipsy violinist?'

'Is there anything madam would particularly like to hear?' asked the waiter as he emerged from the kitchen with a violin and bow in his hand.

'Not just now, thank you,' grinned Nigel.

'Then I'll get on with laying the table, sir.' The waiter sounded rather disappointed. 'Unless you'd prefer to dine in the bedroom?'

Belinda snatched the tablecloth from his free hand and spread it negatively on the table.

'No,' said Nigel. 'I think we're eating in here.'

But the best-laid plans of mice and men, as Oliver might have remarked, often go astray. And sometimes work out exactly how they were meant to. Whichever viewpoint might be taken, it was certain that the events of that night would have stirred in Oliver bitter memories of Binky Heyhoe's sister Candida. In this instance, as far as Oliver was concerned, ignorance was bliss.

Midmorning sunshine shone upon matching bathrobes as Belinda and Nigel breakfasted together in the way people do who have just spent a night together and enjoyed it.

Apart from one thing which Nigel was just then mentioning.

'Look, darling,' he said, 'if you're still worrying about your old man, use the blower.'

'I don't know what to tell him,' Belinda said nervously.

'Tell him the truth,' suggested Nigel a fraction unrealistically.

'Oh, good idea,' Belinda complimented, pulling a face as she mimed a telephone conversation. 'Sorry I didn't come home last night, Daddy, but I got rather tiddly and ended up in bed with Nigel . . . Are you all right, Daddy? What was that funny thump? Sounded like a body hitting the floor.'

She looked helplessly at Nigel who said, 'It's high time he realized that you're a grown-up.'

'I know it is,' agreed a wistful Belinda.

'There's nothing to stop us having breakfast together every morning,' he said seriously.

'You aren't trying to make an honest woman of me, are you?' Belinda wondered.

'Leave it out.' Nigel was not yet ready for so drastic a step. 'I just mean there's plenty of room up at the Grange.'

'What about Daddy?' asked Belinda.

'Not that much room!' he said quickly.

'Nigel!'

'You'll be able to visit him every day,' Nigel assured her. 'You'll still be able to do his cleaning and washing and ironing.' He faced her, his features serious. 'Look, every little bird has to leave the nest sometime, even you.'

'I know,' said Belinda reluctantly. 'But . . .'

'He rips you off!' Seeking to persuade her, Nigel became urgent. 'Look, love, you aren't getting any younger.'

'You silver-tongued charmer, you,' snorted Belinda, knowing that what he said made sense but still afraid to hear it because it might push her into a move she wanted and was afraid to take.

'And neither am I,' he continued. 'I've got forty-seven grey hairs, Belinda. I can't wait forever.'

'I see,' said Belinda, thinking he was joking.

'In fact,' he went on, 'I need a decision by Friday.'

'What's so special about Friday?' Belinda was no longer sure he was joking.

'Well,' said Nigel casually, 'on Saturday I'm flying to Montserrat to finish the album.'

'Where?' She was very frightened now. And frightened to show it.

'Montserrat. Little island in the West Indies.'

'How nice for you.' Hurt: this was unfair pressure.

'Yeah, lovely place.' Nigel smiled reminiscently. 'Palm trees. Blue seas. Golden sands.'

'Sounds like a chocolate box commercial,' Belinda said crossly.

'Right,' agreed Nigel. 'So if you want to come along, you got till Wednesday to sort out your eight fave gramophone records. Here, you have got a passport?'

It suddenly occurred to him that someone who regarded Dorking as a big night out might not have seen much need to obtain the means of leaving the country. It suddenly occurred to Belinda that he wasn't talking about leaving her behind.

'I can get one,' she said confidently.

And they lived happily ever after. Or might have done, had there not been certain other factors to consider, of a nature stoutly opposed to any such fairytale ending. Belinda returned to the cottage in Churston Deckle later that morning to beard one of those factors in his den, which in this instance turned out to be the hall because Oliver was there making a call to the local constabulary.

'Of course she's been kidnapped,' he was declaring. 'And I can name the guilty party!'

'Hello, Daddy,' said Belinda nervously.

Oliver hung up and glowered at her.

'Where the bloody hell do you think you've been?'

Belinda eyed him warily, plucking up her courage. 'I'm sorry if you were worried, but . . .'

'Worried?' Oliver interrupted. 'I've just told the police you've been kidnapped. They said there was no reason to suspect foul play. I said they didn't know Cochrane!'

Belinda went past him into the drawing room, wondering how to broach the subject of her imminent departure. Knowing the reaction did not make it easy. Nor did thirty-three years spent as 'Mr Purcell's Belinda'. Oliver's natural suspicions, however, this time proven well-founded, afforded her the means.

'No doubt,' he said, 'you passed a night of sordid debauchery in some expensive Chelsea hideaway?'

It was a remarkably accurate observation. 'Daddy,' said Belinda, 'you're psychic.'

'You shameless minx!' Oliver was almost, but not quite, too shocked to speak. 'You're not too old to have your legs slapped!'

'Yes I am!' Belinda was angry that he should treat her like a child and angry with herself for feeling guilty. 'I'm a grown woman, for heaven's sake!'

'Is that all you have to say for yourself?' demanded an unplacated and unconvinced Oliver.

'No, it isn't all,' said Belinda, deciding that there was no time like the present for facing up to the inevitable. 'Daddy, there comes a time when a child has to start acting like an adult, or she can't complain if she's treated like an infant.'

'Does that mean he . . .?' Oliver was aghast.

'No,' said Belinda, plucking up all her courage. 'It means *we*.'

'But the man's a . . . a . . .' Oliver sought the right word and was dumbfounded to find he couldn't find it.

Belinda pressed her point. 'Please,' she said, 'I'm very fond of Nigel, and you cannot imagine how tiresome I find your continual sneering and sniping. You don't want me ever to make a life of my own, do you?'

'No,' said Oliver sincerely, 'not with that semi-literate, long-haired street Arab.'

'Save it for the editor of *The Times*, Daddy,' sighed Belinda.

'Remember the fifth commandment, Belinda,' intoned Oliver in his finest patriarchal manner. 'As long as you're living under my roof.'

Whereupon Belinda deflated his pomposity with the simple observation, 'There are other roofs, Daddy.'

'Oh, going to run away from home now, are we?' sneered her father.

'Nigel has asked me to move in with him.'

'You mean,' gasped Oliver in a hushed voice, 'live in sin?'

'As Queen Victoria would have put it,' confirmed Belinda to Oliver's horror, 'Yes.'

'And have you agreed?' Oliver wavered in a voice that suggested he was defeated.

'I told him I'd think it over,' said Belinda. 'On the 'plane to Montserrat.'

Oliver's jaw dropped. This was open rebellion. This was the climax of all his fears from the moment he had first learnt that Belinda was consorting with that damn' singer. This was change and decay run rampant. Oliver's shoulders slumped in defeat. He retreated to the familiarity of his conservatory, where no one answered back.

While Belinda bearded her *bête noire* Nigel prepared to break the news to Lem, who might not, he felt, welcome her company on the island. He found his faithful roadie playing cacophanously at the synthesizer. 'What on earth do you call that row?' was not, perhaps, the best way to start the conversation.

'Well,' said Lem defensively, 'if Belinda can write an album track . . .'

'But Belinda is musically trained,' Nigel pointed out. 'And . . . naturally creative.'

'Ah!' Lem saw instantly through the smile on Nigel's face. 'So you finally scored, eh? At long last!'

'I don't know what you mean,' Nigel said every bit as primly as might Belinda.

'"I don't know what you mean",' snorted Lem, flexing a suggestive arm. 'You and Belinda? All night in your riverside penthouse? Oh boy! What was she like?'

'Lem,' said Nigel warningly. 'Just once – cut it out!'

'I thought so,' Lem crowed. 'I told you didn't I? Now maybe you'll get her out of your system and life can return to normal.'

'Right!' snapped Nigel, upset by these casual references to the object of his devotion. 'Business, Lem.'

'Business,' agreed Lem, subdued by Nigel's obvious irritation.

'Lem,' said Nigel, 'about Montserrat . . .'

'Yeah, I can hardly wait.' The prospect retrieved Lem's natural good humour. 'While you're sweating away in the studio, I'll be out there on the sun-kissed sand, dipping my toes in the Caribbean, giving it plenty of the old coconut oil, strutting my stuff with them beautiful dusky maidens. Oiling their coconuts for them . . .'

'Lem,' Nigel interrupted the happy flow, 'I've asked Belinda to come with us.'

The flow ceased abruptly. Lem said, 'You've gotta be joking,' in a voice that said he was afraid Nigel wasn't.

'That's how I want it, Lem,' said Nigel, confirming as Belinda had confirmed Oliver's, Lem's worst fears.

'Oh, magic!' moaned Lem as the dusky maidens faded. 'I suppose you'll be inviting her to Henry's shindig on Wednesday night.'

'That's a good idea. That's very thoughtful of you, Lem. I'll give her a ring now.'

Nigel picked up the telephone as Lem stared, aghast as Oliver at the prospect of changing circumstances.

Nigel might have considered inviting Belinda to Henry's party a good idea, but that was an opinion largely influenced by his feelings for her and his desire, stemming from those feelings, to introduce her to his world. Which was very different from hers. Belinda might be eager to break away from the conservative confines of Churston Deckle, but most of her life had been passed there and its attitudes and mores had, inevitably, brushed off on her. Excited by the prospect of visiting a nightclub for the first time in her life she purchased a new outfit for the first time in longer than she cared to remember and then found herself wondering why she had bothered. Taking Longfellows as touchstone, and in the absence of any other means of comparison she had to, nightclubs were dark, hot and noisy with the kind of music she didn't enjoy and the kind of people she didn't quite approve of. The majority of Nigel's friends seemed more like Lem than Nigel, and even Nigel, mixing with them, seemed less like himself, or at least less like the Nigel she had fallen for. Henry, whose relationship to Nigel appeared to be that of business manager, was especially obnoxious, a loud and vulgar man at whose table, as chief guest and chief guest's girlfriend, they were obliged to sit. Belinda wanted to go home.

'So I said,' said Henry through the noise and the smoke, 'Cochrane's gonna be bigger than Graf Spee ever were, so if two million is your best offer, you can take your three album deal and shove it up your back catalogue!'

'Bit strong, weren't it?' commented Nigel, and called to a bespectacled waiter, 'Oy, four eyes! How about some more champagne? This ain't a bleedin' temperance meeting, you know.'

'Nigel,' hissed Belinda disapprovingly, 'don't be so rude.'

Nigel ignored her as Henry continued, 'At least I got us a cracking deal on the video rights. Didn't I, Sharon?'

Sharon was an attractive and, Belinda assumed as so far she hadn't said a word, dumb blonde. Had she been about to say something was anyone's guess because just then Lem strolled up with a taller, blonder, even more attractive blonde and said, 'Here, meet Kinsey.'

Kinsey could speak. She said, 'Hi.'

'She's a model,' explained Lem.

'Really?' Belinda smiled with acid politeness. 'In this light she looks almost the real thing.'

The comment went unnoticed by the pair, who sat down and proceeded to neck voraciously. Someone engaged the garrulous Henry in conversation and Belinda took the opportunity to catch Nigel's attention.

'When are we going?'

'In a minute.' He sounded in no hurry and couldn't leave then anyway because a wavy-haired young man with a languid air wandered over to ask, 'Nigel, how goes it?'

'Not so bad,' said Nigel coolly.

'Just had to come over and tell you I saw you in Leicester,' enthused the stranger. 'You're much better without the band.'

'Oh yeah?' It didn't sound as though he cared much for the young man's opinion.

'Yeah, really great,' confirmed the newcomer and wandered off again.

'Who was that?' Belinda asked.

'Dunno.' Nigel shrugged, the young man already dismissed from his thoughts as he had been dismissed from the table. 'Some bootlicker. One of Henry's young hopefuls.'

In the strobe stroked darkness of the nightclub Belinda began to see Nigel in a new light. And was not sure she liked what she saw. But she had no opportunity to say or do anything because just then Henry leant across the table to say, 'Oh, Nige, there's Tricia Rembrandt over there. Go and chat her up – she might have you on her telly programme.'

Nigel promptly stood up and left Belinda alone with Henry and Sharon as he crossed to the bar to greet a well-preserved woman like a long-lost friend. Or, thought Belinda, something more. Any speculation in this area was lost together with the chance of observing the meeting by Henry's attentions.

'Hello, beautiful.' He leant a lot closer to Belinda. 'I'm Henry. Sorry I ain't had the chance to say hello properly before.'

'I quite understand, Henry,' said Belinda in her best Home Counties voice, 'we've only been sitting next to each other for two and a half hours.'

This sally left Henry quite undeterred. 'Sharp!' he commented, nudging his wife to draw her attention from her chewing gum to Belinda. 'Here, Sharon, Lem said she was sharp, and she is. Been looking forward to meeting you. Having a good time?'

'It's been,' allowed Belinda, 'very interesting.'

'Nigel tells me you're a bit of a song-writer.' Henry smiled, sucking on a cigar.

'Well, barely.' Belinda blushed modestly, flattered.

''Cos I wouldn't be averse to handling you, if you get my drift.'

It was a trifle early for Belinda to have considered the need for a business manager, but that was not necessarily, it occurred to her, what Henry was talking about because Sharon tugged at his arm and whispered something in his ear that brought him smiling oilily back to Belinda.

'Here,' he suggested, putting an unwanted arm around her shoulders, 'how about you and Nige coming back with Shar and me later and playing some party games?'

'I don't think Nigel plays bridge,' was her excuse.

'Did I say sharp?' Henry hooted. 'Should have said cruel! No, the sort of game I was thinking of . . .'

As he explained the arm around Belinda's shoulders moved farther and lower. Belinda's face paled and her mouth dropped open as the details were unfolded. 'How dare you?' she gasped. 'I'm going!'

'Come on, doll, I'm Nigel's manager,' said Henry as though this justified all. Which in Henry's opinion it obviously did. 'I'm in for fifteen per cent of whatever he's making if you catch my drift. It's centrally heated.'

Not even this advantage could persuade Belinda. She rose with icy dignity and stalked from the table towards the exit, missing Nigel as he returned from his interview-finding mission.

'Guess who's going to get a profile on BBC2 then?' He noticed his beloved was gone and frowned. 'Where's Belinda? Oy, Lem.'

Lem unglued his mouth from Kinsey's just long enough to tell him, 'She's split. I told you this weren't her scene, Nige.'

'Bit strait-laced, ain't she?' Henry pointed towards the exit. 'Lem told me she likes a bit of rough.'

'Oh, did he?' Nigel's gaze was poisonous as it turned balefully on a cheerfully oblivious roadie. But Lem was saved from immediate retribution by the sight of Belinda arguing with a bored cloakroom attendant.

'It's perfectly obvious which is my coat,' she was saying. 'My name tag is sewn in the collar.'

'Sorry, love.' This announcement made no difference to the girl. 'No ticket, no coat. I mean, I don't make the rules.'

'What's up?' asked Nigel as he arrived on the scene.

'You really don't know?' snapped Belinda.

'Look, it was all Lem's idea of a joke.' Nigel was torn between the need to apologize and instinctive defence of his friends. 'Henry's all right, really.'

'What about you and that middle-aged floozie?' demanded an unplacated Belinda.

'That was just business,' said Nigel innocently. 'We was talking about her giving me a special.'

The ambiguity of the statement prompted Belinda to kick him on the shin. Hard. 'So I saw.'

'What was that for?' Nigel winced, rubbing his assaulted leg. 'Look, I've got to chat up all these people. It's work.'

'They're revolting!' Belinda was beginning to wonder if their worlds weren't too far apart for any kind of relationship to be possible. 'And what's worse, when you're with them you're like them.'

'Belinda,' he pleaded, 'we aren't that bad. Look, in Montserrat you'll have a chance to get to know them better.'

'Those perverts are coming to Montserrat?'

Visions of a sun-kissed paradise vanished, palm trees, golden sand and clear blue sea replaced by the image of Henry and sundry multiples locked in unspeakable obscenities. Robinson Crusoe and Friday joined by Saturday, Sunday, Monday, Tuesday, Wednesday and Thursday.

'Can't finish the album without them,' shrugged Nigel.

'Then I wish,' said Belinda stiffly, 'to withdraw my application for the position of concubine.'

And she swept coatless from the nightclub, leaving a sheepish Nigel with two cloakroom tickets in his hand and an empty seat on the 'plane.

Like a motorway, the path of true love seldom runs smooth, but Belinda had hardly anticipated so drastic an upheaval. A bump or two, perhaps, but not so final a parting. Indeed, no parting at all; it had seemed a little early to think of partings when they had only just, to put it euphemistically, got together. But there it was: culture clash in a big way. Disco versus concert hall. Montserrat with Henry versus Churston Deckle with Oliver. And it looked as though Oliver had won in the long run.

'To think Nigel's only been gone a week, Vincent,' she told the rubber plant wistfully. 'But of course, a week's a long time to a rubber plant. Oh, a new leaf! Well done.'

She was beginning to sound like Oliver who now appeared, wheeling his chair into the conservatory with a tray across the arms to announce, 'I've made you a nice fresh cup of coffee, Belinda.'

'Thank you, Daddy.' Her voice was dutiful and dull.

Oliver did his best to cheer her: 'If the weather holds, we might go for a little walk this afternoon.'

'It was eighty-seven degrees Fahrenheit in Montserrat yesterday,' she murmured thoughtfully.

'Much too hot,' said Oliver gruffly.

'Oh, absolutely,' Belinda agreed listlessly.

'I'll get you a nice chocolate digestive,' suggested a much changed and unusually subdued Oliver, and left the plant-filled room.

Belinda sighed, gazing at Vincent, who took on the

aspect of a palm tree waving gently in the balmy breeze that drifted lazily across the soft, warm sand that banded the calm, blue ocean. Henry was nowhere in sight. But then nor was Nigel. At least, not in Belinda's sight because he was creeping into the conservatory through the back door with Lem and a blanket that he tossed adroitly over her head before sweeping her on to Lem's shoulder and following his laden roadie quickly out.

Oliver returned to an empty room.

'Belle? Your coffee is growing no warmer. Belinda, we played hide and seek yesterday. Oh, very well,' he sighed, giving in to his daughter's womanly whim. Or so he thought, just as he thought she would get over the singer-hooligan soon enough. 'One, two, three, five, nineteen, thirty-two, fifty.'

'Daddy will never pay the ransom,' said Belinda as Lem removed the blanket. She was smiling.

So was Lem as he joked, 'Right, that's it! Wrap her up, Nige. We'll take her back.'

Nigel was smiling too, like a man who hopes he's got what he wants at last. He was leaning against a bank of equipment and Belinda saw that they were in the mastering room at the Grange, recording and playback equipment stacked around them. 'Right. Hope you're gonna like this.' Nigel flicked a switch. 'Because you wrote it.'

As music filled the room a newly-chastened Lem offered discreet excuses to leave. They were accepted.

'Not my Eastbourne song?' Belinda asked.

'But with words.' Nigel tapped his chest to indicate whose. 'I've got seven seconds to get behind the microphone.'

Belinda watched as he stepped inside a soundproofed booth with a window at head height and began to sing . . .

'Last night I told her that I didn't let her down,
But she called me a liar.
Too many nights I just wasn't around
When she burned with desire.'

Belinda rose, crossing to the booth to stare in through the little window.

'Taking her for granted is my sorry excuse,' sang Nigel with a chorus coming in on the closing words.

'Now she's walked right out my door,
What did I go and do?'

Suspecting that all was not as it seemed Belinda slid the door open and stepped inside. Her suspicions were confirmed as Nigel's voice continued, 'Don't you turn your back on the one you love,' while he kissed her.

'You did that without moving your lips,' she said softly.

'Yeah,' said Nigel. And did it again.

A selection of humour titles available in Panther Books

All these books are available at your local bookshop or newsagent, or can be ordered direct from the publisher.,

---

To order direct from the publisher just tick the titles you want and fill in the form below.

Name ____________________

Address ____________________

____

Send to:
Panther Cash Sales
PO Box 11, Falmouth, Cornwall TR10 9EN.

Please enclose remittance to the value of the cover price plus:

UK 45p for the first book, 20p for the second book plus 14p per copy for each additional book ordered to a maximum charge of £1.63.

BFPO and Eire 45p for the first book, 20p for the second book plus 14p per copy for the next 7 books, thereafter 8p per book.

Overseas 75p for the first book and 21p for each additional book.

Panther Books reserve the right to show new retail prices on covers, which may differ from those previously advertised in the text or elsewhere.